"Damn you, Stacia," Paul exclaimed.

"You should know how it is to be near you . . . you should know how you look in the moonlight, with your hair turned silver and your skin silver and your eyes . . ." He broke off. "For God's sake, go inside."

There was a throbbing deep in her throat. There was a growing happiness inside of her; it was keeping pace with her yearning to have him with her. "Paul," she whispered. "Please come back with me . . ."

Dear Reader:

We've had thousands of wonderful surprises at SECOND CHANCE AT LOVE since we launched the line in June 1981.

We knew we were going to have to work hard to bring you the six best romances we could each month. We knew we were working with a talented, caring group of authors. But we *didn't* know we were going to receive such a warm and generous response from readers. So the thousands of wonderful surprises are in the form of letters from readers like you who've been kind with your praise, constructive and helpful with your suggestions. We read each letter...and take it seriously.

It's been a thrill to "meet" our readers, to discover that the people who read SECOND CHANCE AT LOVE novels and write to us about them are so remarkable. Our romances can only get better and better as we learn more and more about you, the reader, and what you like to read.

So, I hope you will continue to enjoy SECOND CHANCE AT LOVE and, if you haven't written to us before, please feel free to do so. If you have written, keep in touch.

With every good wish,

Sincerely,

Carolyn Nichols

Carolyn Nichols
SECOND CHANCE AT LOVE
The Berkley/Jove Publishing Group
200 Madison Avenue
New York, New York 10016

P.S. Because your opinions *are* so important to us, I urge you to fill out and return the questionnaire in the back of this book.

Second Chance at Love™

CACTUS ROSE

ZANDRA COLT

A
SECOND CHANCE AT LOVE
BOOK

chapter

1

STANDING IN THE doorway of the Republic Airlines Office, Stacia Marshall stared across the wide expanse of airfield. She grimaced as she saw the Piper Cub which was to bring her up to Las Vegas for what her fellow journalists were calling "the wedding of the year." She was not in the habit of covering weddings, and certainly she was not in the mood. She turned back, her gaze on the clock centered on the opposite wall. Her glance shifted to her watch. "Well, at least *I'm* here," she said pointedly to Anne Harte, the friend who had insisted on seeing her off. "Where is he?"

Unnecessarily, Anne consulted the golden trifle on her slender tanned wrist. "I make it six of seven," she commented. "He's not supposed to be here until seven. You're obviously thinking of George. Not every man in the world is late for appointments."

Stacia glared at her. "I was *not* thinking of George," she lied.

"And," Anne continued critically, "I don't see why you couldn't have worn something a little more suitable." Complacently, she looked at her own white linen dress, which flattered her slim figure and formed a most agreeable contrast to her dark tan.

Stacia regarded her own faded blue jeans, battered matching jacket, white tee-shirt and sneakers with a sim-

1

ilar complacency, which had just a trace of defiance in it. "These are my *working* clothes," she emphasized. "I am not a guest, Anne, dear; I am there to take pictures of the wedding of Paul Curtis, heir-apparent to Curtis Motors, and his lovely bride-to-be, Gloria Mannon Meade, whose father is the head of Mannon Tires, Inc. And, of course, there will be the launching of the Curtis Foundation. I shall write an ecstatic commentary with the emphasis squarely on romance."

"And Paul Curtis is going to fly you there," Anne breathed, suggesting that she had not been listening as closely to Stacia's bitter remarks as she might.

Stacia swallowed a derisive laugh. Her friend had pronounced the name reverently. If she had possessed any lingering illusions as to Anne's eagerness to see her off, they would have been blasted by the note of wistful longing she heard in her friend's voice. It was just as well that *Eyeview* magazine was not sending Anne Harte to report on the nuptials between Paul "Motors" and Gloria "Tires." It was a pain that *Eyeview's* editor, Dave Lynch, was sending her. Stacia ground her teeth. If she could have gone on one of Paul Curtis's much-publicized mountain-climbing expeditions or accompanied him on his trip down the Amazon river, that, at least, would have been worthwhile, but a society wedding in which two great fortunes were to be joined, presumably to multiply happily ever after or until the participants agreed to disagree and were divorced, was not her idea of a rewarding assignment. That was what she had told Dave. "Why not that 'Tourism in Italy' piece? You promised it to me," she had grumbled.

"You'll have it. The wedding will take no more than a weekend, and when you return, you can go to Italy. This is going to be a change of pace for you, Stacy. The

Curtis family—Mrs. Curtis particularly—is news. You'll do a bang-up job on her. No holds barred."

That was the only good part of the assignment. She would not need to approach the subject reverently, which, she thought derisively, was one more reason why she was being flown to the site by the groom himself. She had had an interview which had kept her from going up to Vegas with the rest of the press in the plane which had also been chartered by Curtis Motors.

"As it happens," Mrs. Curtis had told Dave Lynch, "my son's going to be in San Francisco for the day. He will be able to take Miss Marshall back with him."

Perhaps Mrs. Curtis believed that Stacy would be bowled over by the heir-apparent's celebrated charm. Unfortunately for that publicity-minded lady, Miss Stacia Marshall was George-conditioned against charm. *George*.

It had been seven months, three weeks and two days since George and she had broken up. The wound had healed, but the scar tissue remained. She had a distinct prejudice against men of his ilk—tall, handsome, self-assured, selfish and well connected. If she were ever to become interested in a man again, certainly it would not be in Paul Curtis, who spent his portion of the family millions diving for Greek treasures in the Aegean, skiing down the Alps or climbing up them or going wherever he could garner plenty of publicity. It was one way of keeping Curtis Motors in the news, though she suspected that he was far more interested in keeping Mr. Paul Curtis appropriately spotlighted. How much more admirable to have spent the money endowing a hospital or bringing food to the world's starving children!

"Will it take long to get from here to Vegas?" Anne asked.

"I shouldn't think so," Stacia replied.

"He ought to be here soon. At least comb your hair. It looks like you went through it with an eggbeater."

"Do you have any more props for my self-confidence, dear?"

"If I had hair your color...that golden blond, and your green eyes—such an exciting combination—I would make the most of it. It's all wasted on you. I hope you're not going to wear your 'working clothes' to the wedding!"

"No." Stacia indicated her small canvas tote bag. "I shall flutter forth from my chrysalis, and Paul Curtis, in the midst of repeating his vows, will come to a stop—glance in my direction and say, 'Ah, divinely fair maiden, where have you been all my life?'—and leave Gloria flat...a flat *tire.*"

Anne laughed. "I don't say you should have designs on the groom. He's not going to be the only man present. The flower of America's manhood undoubtedly will be there."

"And wilting." Stacia nodded. "Vegas in June."

"It's only the first of June."

"No matter—it will be hot." Stacia emitted a short laugh. "George doesn't like hot weather."

"George! You're not suggesting that he'll be there."

"He's on the guest list. Mr. and Mrs. George Lansing, Jr."

"Oh, God." Anne paled. "What will you do?"

"Shoot them." Stacia laughed at Anne's startled glance and pointed to the Nikon she had slung around her neck.

"Miss Marshall?"

Stacia turned to see a tall man in brown—brown pants, brown suede jacket, brown shirt. His skin was also brown, the tan broadcasting the long hours he'd spent basking on the beaches of the world. His dark eyes were fastened on Anne, admiringly, too admiringly for one who was soon to exchange binding vows with Gloria Mannon Meade. Anne, Stacia noted, looked back at him as if he were a large stretch of Promised Land. Regretfully, Anne said, "No, this is Miss Marshall. I'm Anne Harte."

"Hi," Stacia said. "You're Mr. Curtis?"

He regarded her disinterestedly. "Yes. Hello."

His appearance depressed Stacia. It would be easy to photograph him—too easy. From all angles, he was handsome. He had well-shaped features, his brown eyes were flecked with gold, his hair was wavy. It would be hard not to do justice to that face, but she was going to make the effort. She could catch him off guard—in the act of eating, so that his mouth would be open. People always looked foolish with their mouths open. They could look equally foolish when they were talking, if you happened to focus in on them at the right moment. She was an expert at finding the right moments. In the *Eye-view* files were numerous hate letters, all from subjects she had photographed. She was really going to do a job on Mr. Paul Curtis, who was even more attractive than George. Two years ago, pre-George, when she was still fancy-free, she would probably have envied his bride. Now—no holds barred, that was the ticket!

"Well," Mr. Curtis said, his eyes on Anne, "I expect we'd better be on our way."

Stacia nodded. "Okay."

"Where's your luggage, Miss Marshall?"

"Here." She indicated her tote bag.

He picked it up. "You go on out to the plane. I've got to check on things. It's that one. . . ." He indicated the Piper Cub.

Stacia and Anne walked outside. "Divine," Anne muttered.

"Absolutely," Stacia said mockingly.

"He was right on time," Anne reminded her. "God, to think of all that opportunity wasted on you. I wish you could remember that every man is not George."

"Tell that to Gloria Mannon Meade."

"I wish I were in your place."

"So, I am sure, does he. Though what even you could accomplish in a short hop to Las Vegas—and with his hands on the controls of the plane—I am not sure. As far as I'm concerned, I would be much happier in a commercial airliner."

"He's flown around the world more than once by himself, and don't forget that it was a commercial airliner that your parents—Oh, God." Anne broke off, flushing. "I didn't mean to remind you . . ."

Stacia winced, but she said merely, "That's all right, but I can tell you truthfully that I wish to the good Lord you were in my place with the too, too charismatic and handsome Mr. Paul Curtis-millions."

"'If wishes were horses, beggars would ride,'" a cool voice behind them remarked.

"Oh!" Anne whirled.

Stacia faced Paul Curtis calmly. "Are we about to take off, then?"

"You guessed it, Miss Marshall. Your time has come."

"Oh, heavens, I hope you didn't mean that the way it sounded." Anne giggled nervously.

"I am confident that we will arrive safely and on time," he returned. The smile that twisted his lips, however, was mirthless, and his eyes were cold. Evidently, Stacia thought with some satisfaction, surprise had sent the fabled Curtis charm into momentary eclipse. She guessed it must be a new sensation for him to meet at least one woman who remained unimpressed by rampant masculinity on the hoof.

"Well," Anne said, "I guess it's time to bid you good-bye. Happy landings."

"Thanks, Miss Harte." He clasped her outstretched hand. His eyes were warm again, his smile genuine. He had no trouble dealing with the Anne Hartes of this world. He understood them perfectly, Stacia thought.

She turned to Anne. "Thanks for seeing me off, dear. I'll call when I arrive."

"Do. Have a wonderful time, Stacia." Moving closer, Anne embraced her, whispering urgently, "Try and be a little more pleasant. He's nice. And remove those damned dark glasses. They make you look like a panda!"

As Paul Curtis brought the plane into position for takeoff, Stacia, looking out of the window, hoped that Anne, now a small white figure in the distance, could see her dark glasses. She was really rather annoyed with her friend. The man at the controls did not need the unabashed admiration with which she had colored her every look, gesture and remark. Well, at least, she, Stacia Marshall, had proved that she was not situated on that same wave length. She had not intended him to overhear her sarcastic comments, but since he had, it was just as well.

Evidently, he had also decided that, mother or no mother, he was not going to try and mend matters between them. He, for one, was evidently not afraid of what *Eyeview* might print. Unfortunately, she thought ruefully, he did not have to worry about *Eyeview*—there would be dozens of articles that would neutralize anything she could etch in her own particular brand of acid.

Consequently, when he had helped her into the plane, his sole comment before settling down at the controls had been, "Fasten your seat belt, Miss Marshall."

The seat was small and narrow, but she was not sorry to be sitting down. Her day had been hectic. She had risen at five and written an article, which she had sent to her home office, in New York. She had finished about noon and dashed out to Sausalito for an interview with a rock group called the Sausa Seven, returning at five. She had stopped off at her San Francisco pied-à-terre, packed and driven across town to pick up Anne, who was to drive her car back. And this was actually the first moment she had had to relax. She blinked. In spite of the gibberish coming out of the squawk box, in spite of the loud drone of the motor and in spite of her own fears about traveling in this small craft, she was feeling unexpectedly drowsy. It was not her habit to sleep on planes. Though she hadn't given up air travel, she had never been totally relaxed since her mother and father had gone down in the Aegean Sea. She shuddered, not wanting to think of that. Putting her head back, she closed her eyes.

"Oh, damn!" Paul Curtis's exclamation, loud and breathless . . . a sense of shaking from side to side . . . the droning of the motor changing to spasmodic coughs . . . a shrill whistling in her ears and the metal buckle of her seat belt hard against her stomach were some of the fragmented impressions that traveled through Stacia's mind as she awakened. These were replaced by cold fear. Something was wrong! Something was happening to the plane. She leaned forward, crying out questions to the man in front of her, who could not hear her, because he was jiggling the controls, was calling into the radio, was leaning forward himself, peering through the window.

A swift descent, a bump, air rushing in, something tearing loose—a sense of falling forward, of a sharp pain in her foot, of things sticking into her, of a crackling in her ears—more pain, darkness, nothing.

An acrid scent of gasoline was in her nostrils—no, not gasoline: fuel, plane fuel. She had dreamed that the plane had fallen. It was natural she would dream that—considering what had happened to her parents. Stacia opened her eyes, and high above her shone the moon. That was peculiar. She would have thought the moon would be in a different position since they, too, were in the sky.

"I wonder why it's not," she said distinctly.

"Ah, you're awake."

She tensed. Who had spoken? The voice was vaguely familiar, but at the moment she could not place it. George? No, not George. He was married and back in New York or Capri or Sardinia, wherever the fashionable jetted to. She could not think of the name of the person who belonged to the voice. It did not matter. She tried to move, and everything ached and stung and throbbed.

"Don't move. We'll need to wait until it's light. Just lie still."

There was a quaver in that voice—as if it were weary or tearful—and, of course, it was a man's voice, or she would not have thought of George. Paul Curtis? *Yes.* She had exchanged only a few words with him, but it was his voice, a deep rich, baritone, very pleasant to the ear . . . but that did not matter. Something had happened to the plane. She had not dreamed it. She was annoyed with herself for not understanding immediately.

"We crashed, didn't we, Mr. Curtis?"

"Yes."

"How?"

"Musn't talk so much. Tomorrow...in daylight...easier to sort things out..." His voice was slurred as if he were drunk, but that could also indicate shock.

"Are you hurt?" she whispered, trying to raise herself.

"Not much." A gentle hand was on her shoulder, pushing her back. "Lie still."

Strangely, she felt very tired again. "I'm sleepy," she muttered.

"Good."

"Why?"

"'Chief nourisher in life's feast.'"

"Shakespeare..." she whispered.

"Head of the class, Miss Marshall."

She could not answer. Weariness washed over her. She did not really want to sleep; she wanted to know how it had happened—the crash—but she would not be able to comprehend the answers. She was not sure why she was so certain of that. She felt something soft descend on her and wondered what it was. She was having a dreadful time trying to concentrate. In fact, there was no use trying, no use fighting the darkness lurking behind her descending eyelids....

chapter

2

IT WAS LIGHT. It was well beyond dawn. The sky was cloudy, but a sporadic sunshine filtered through the furred branches of the tall pine tree. It sparkled on what appeared to be bits of metal or glass but, Stacia decided, were actually rocks and pebbles which must have a quartz content.

She blinked against the reflected light, and her eyelids hurt. Her body was one mass of aches and pains, and it smarted. It had taken considerable effort for her to drag herself to the tree and prop herself against its trunk. Fortunately, she had always possessed great stores of willpower.

"Stubbornness," her mother had called it.

"Determination," her father had said, tempering the definition.

She preferred his definition. She was thinking of her parents, thinking that she had almost joined them in death. She realized that now, realized just what had happened. She had understood the night before, but it was much clearer now. The plane had gone down while she was sleeping. With a little shudder, she realized she might have slept her way into death, but miraculously, she had survived the crash, and, she thought, in one piece. She did not believe she had broken any bones. She could move even though her ankle was swollen to twice its normal size—still she diagnosed it as a sprain, not a break. The sun was brighter now. She squinted, wishing she had not lost her dark glasses. Glasses. She looked down at her chest and discovered that her Nikon was missing. She winced. That was a pain, a different sort of pain, but a pain nonetheless. She loved that camera. How had it dropped off her neck? Maybe, she thought hopefully, Paul Curtis had removed it.

She tensed. Where was he? Vaguely, she remembered someone speaking to her sometime in the night. She could not remember what had been said, but it must have been he who had spoken. Or had she only dreamed it? She glanced down and saw the suede jacket that had been over her when she had awakened. That was his jacket. She remembered it. Brown. He had been wearing brown—and where was he?

Stacia looked about her and saw only the trunks of trees, and on the ground, among the glistening rocks, pine needles and pine cones. What had happened to him? Was he still asleep, or maybe hurt or . . . worse? No, it was ridiculous to think along those lines. It must have been Paul Curtis who had said whatever had been said to her during the night. The jacket was there to prove that Paul Curtis, the pilot who had steered them into a mountain, still existed in this world. Or was it a mountain? It might be a forest. That did not matter at this moment. How had the plane happened to go down? The weather? Engine trouble? The pilot. She tensed. Human error. His error. Very likely. In all probability! Naturally. She had not wanted to fly with him. It had been against her better judgement. She drew a long breath and expelled it in a short, angry sigh. She had had no choice. Yes, she had had a choice; she could have gone tomorrow on a regular airline. What had made her decide to accept

Mrs. Curtis's offer? Private planes, piloted by amateurs! She must have been crazy. She remembered Anne's remark about his flying around the world. Luck? Undoubtedly. She should have gone to the damned wedding in the morning. What had possessed her?

Dave Lynch had possessed her. "It'll be a chance to get a real insight into him, love."

She had possessed herself. She had agreed with her editor. She could admit to being curious as to what made Mr. Paul "Motors" Curtis tick. She recalled the rumor that he was taking over the reins of the company from Mama Curtis. She recalled not believing it. Mama Curtis was the brains, blood and sinew behind Curtis Motors. She was a legend in her own time: a noted sportswoman—tennis, gold, horses—who knew the assembly line as well as the front office. There was even a tale she, Stacia, almost believed, that Mama Curtis could supervise the making of a Curtmotor from drawing board to road test, even to the insertion of nuts and bolts. Whether the story was true or not, she had been in the driver's seat of Curtis Motors ever since the death of Paul Livingston Curtis, twenty years earlier, when her son was only ten. Was she ready, willing and able to become the Dowager Empress? That was a question Stacia had been burning to ask the heir-apparent. And that's why she had trusted her life to this . . . this shirt ad. She paused in her thinking. Her grandmother had had a contempt for handsome, useless men. "Shirt ad" had been her expression, and it had certainly fitted George. Mr. Curtis, she suspected, was another George. She had put her happiness on the line for George Lansing, Jr., and she had put her life on the line for Paul Curtis, Jr.—and all for that damned wedding!

Wedding!

She glanced at her watch. Predictably, it was still running. Its hands pointed to eight. Eight in the morning of June first. The ceremony was scheduled for high noon. She could envision the confusion, the consternation, the fear and the grief.

She could see Gloria Mannon Meade staring blindly at her wedding gown. Every detail of that gown, a Halston creation, had been described in fashion columns throughout the fifty states. It had been featured in *Harper's Bazaar* and had figured in a color spread in *Time*. But why on earth was she thinking about wedding gowns? Gloria would not be mourning a dress; she would be mourning a bridegroom. How the media would be milking the situation. Naturally, everybody must think they were dead!

There would be big black headlines in the newspapers: CURTIS HEIR CRASHES! Television would be full of the story, and the radio would, too. It would be a news break twice as big as the wedding itself—and she, Stacia Marshall, had the inside track—no holds barred. She laughed dryly and wished she hadn't, because it made her chest ache. The irony of her situation would have to be appreciated in silence. Rather than tracking down a story, she was in the cast of characters. However, after they were rescued, she would certainly be able to add her bit to the tale. She glanced up at the sky, almost expecting to see a circling search plane. Well, perhaps it was a little early for that, but they would come. They would scour all territories for them—correction, not for them, for him—for Mr. Paul Curtis.

She jumped as she heard a rustling in the bushes. It sounded as if something were making its way through them. Bushes? Where were there bushes? She could only see tree trunks. There was one directly in front of her, blocking her vision, but it was bereft of branches—a twisted trunk, lightning-struck, probably.

The rustling sound was coming nearer. What lurked in forests? Or more specifically, pine forests? Squirrels, snakes, bears...was it a bear sound she was hearing? Belatedly, she remembered that bears were to be found in Sequoia National Park. They might have landed near Sequoia or Tahoe or Mount Baldy or...A shadow fell across the clearing. It was not the shadow of a bear. It was, of course, the shadow of a man—Paul Curtis.

He came slowly toward her, clutching low-hanging pine branches as he passed among them. Finally, he stopped, breathing hard and leaning gratefully against that lightning-blasted tree trunk.

Stacia looked at him in amazement and realized in that moment that she had been expecting to see the man of the airport, handsome, self-assured, impeccably turned out in brown. Instead, he looked more like an shadow of his former self. He was covered the grease, dirt and blood. His shirt was torn at the shoulder; his trousers were ripped on one side from knee to ankle. His cheek was cut, blood from a wound near his temple had trickled down the side of his face and his dark hair was matted and glistening with sweat. If she had not been so resentful, she might have felt sorry for him, but her eyes told her that there was no real reason for that. His wounds were superficial, and he was walking, which was something she might not be able to do for a week!

He looked at her, concern in his expression. "You should not have sat up, Miss Marshall'..." He paused to catch his breath. "You don't know the extent of your injuries."

"I'm okay," she said shortly. "How about you?"

"Nothing much...a few surface scratches. Naturally,

I got shaken up. Still, we were very lucky." His mouth twisted. "At least, I hope we were."

She did not try to understand what he meant by that. She had another, more pressing question. "What happened to the plane?"

"I'm afraid its injuries are beyond repair," he said grimly. "I've been tinkering with it, but to no avail."

That, she thought wryly, was not surprising, considering the talent on hand, but maybe he did deserve A for effort. The hell he did! D minus was more like it. "I shouldn't think it would be in very good working order after last night," she said. "What I meant is—what caused the accident in the first place?"

"Engine trouble. I'll have plenty to tell that damned mechanic."

"That damned mechanic," she repeated to herself. Easy to blame him. She wondered how often Mr. Paul Curtis had shifted the burden of his responsibilities onto the shoulders of some anonymous menial. "Maybe it would have been better to have done your telling before we left," she said coldly.

"What does that mean?" he inquired.

"We took off only minutes after you got to the airfield. Maybe you were thinking of other things?"

He frowned. "You're suggesting that I didn't have the plane checked before departure time? For your information, Miss Marshall, I always have the engine checked thoroughly when I am taking the plane up. Any intelligent pilot does that."

"I had always thought so." She tinctured her words with the sarcasm which had become habitual to her since George-time.

He favored her with an icy stare. "I can see that you think it's my fault we're in this trouble."

"It had crossed my mind," she murmured.

"I assure you..." He paused. "No, never mind, Believe what you like, Miss Marshall. It doesn't matter, and I am not about to try to justify myself in your eyes. That, I think, was a lost cause from the very beginning. It doesn't surprise me—after all, you are representative of the sort of talent employed by *Eyeview*."

She bristled. "And I am proud of it! It's a damned good magazine."

"It is a salacious, scandal-mongering, muckraking piece of crap, staffed by writers with a post-graduate degree in bitchery. And why my mother was so eager to have me make a special trip down to Frisco to get you is beyond me. I told her so at the time."

"I was told you were in San Francisco on business," Stacia stated.

"You were that business. And if you're wondering why that wasn't made plain to you, Mother was fearful you'd think of it as some sort of gesture of appeasement."

"And wasn't it?" she inquired sweetly.

He regarded her through narrowed eyes. "I'm not going to continue this sparring. You might be primed for fighting, but I'm not. I've got other matters on my mind, such as how we're going to make it back to civilization."

"Civilization?" she repeated, tensing and instinctively recoiling from the implications of his observation. She was unwillingly reminded of the question which, she realized, had been hovering at the brink of her mind ever since she had opened her eyes. She had contemplated it briefly, but she had pushed it away as something to be dealt with at a later time. There was no reason to ignore it any longer. It needed to be asked. "Where are we, Mr. Curtis?"

"Off hand, I'd say we're somewhere in the Sierra Nevada mountains."

"That had occurred to me, too, but *where?* I expect

you've learned our position from the squawk box?"

"Unfortunately, I was too concerned with the business of righting the aircraft and making some sort of a landing to pay attention to the squawk box, as you call it. By the time I'd made it to the bushes where we came down, the radio had shorted out. Please spare me your comments on my lack of forethought. I am aware of my errors and I take full blame for them."

A number of choice remarks trembled on her tongue, but she restrained them. It wouldn't have done any good to unburden herself on the subject of his total incompetence or suggest that it might have been better if Mrs. Curtis had piloted the plane herself. It would only have made matters worse between them, if that were possible. She could only hope that they would not be thrust into each other's company for long—but it went without saying that they were in a ghastly situation. Not only had they crash-landed; they might be in some impenetrable forest vastness where they could wander about for days until . . . She did not want to think about the possibilities, not yet. Glancing up, she met his ironic gaze.

"Thank you for your restraint, Miss Marshall," he remarked, sinking down and propping himself against the dead tree. He had moved stiffly, carefully, and Stacia had the impression he was in pain. Probably that was why he was sitting there—near her—because he could not stand any longer. It was too late to ask any questions concerning his injuries. He would not welcome such inquiries from her. He did not like her any more than she liked him, and, correspondingly, his prejudices had been formed before their meeting. Obviously, he believed all *Eyeview* staffers came from the same mold, and she had become accustomed to comparing all men of his type to George. That didn't matter. Nor did it matter that they weren't slated to be soul mates. All that mattered was getting back, but even if their exact position was unknown, there would be search planes.

"They'll come looking for you," she said.

"They be looking for us *both*," he replied emphatically. He looked up at the pine tree. "That's a ponderosa," he commented.

"Ponderosa? What's that?"

"A species of pine tree."

"Oh." She nodded. She was unable to keep from adding sarcastically, "I see you're a naturalist."

"I know something about trees in this part of the country. Pines grow at different levels in the mountains. If you can tell one species from the other, you've an inkling as to what level you're on."

"I see." She flushed, feeling remarkably foolish. "And at what level does this tree grow?"

"If I'm right about it's being a ponderosa, and I'm pretty sure I am, we might be near the foothills. Ponderosa forests grow farther down. You find them around the old mining camps—gold country. That'd be a very good place to have landed. We'd be running into hikers, backpackers—maybe a ranger station."

"Do you suppose that's where we are?" she asked eagerly.

"I'm not sure. Sometimes the trees are mixed. A coniferous pine forest grows about three thousand feet up—near Lake Tahoe, for instance. That wouldn't be a bad place to have come down, either."

"No, certainly not," she agreed. Another question occurred to her, one which she was reluctant to even consider, much less ask. "We—we could be higher up, too, couldn't we?"

He jerked his thumb at a tree growing a few feet away. "Red firs like that one grow seven thousand feet up."

"Oh, God, what if—"

"Don't think, don't speculate, don't wonder," he advised crisply. "We need to take these things a step at a time. You look at the whole spectrum and you miss the small details. Details are where it's at—where we're at."

"Details, yes," she repeated, subduing an angry retort, a reminder that she did not need any advice from him, particularly on the subject of survival. Clothing, food and water—those were the details. She repeated them aloud. "Clothes, food and water?"

"Right, but not in that order."

"Water?"

"Back to the head of the class."

The remark registered as something she had heard before. Where? From him? Yes, last night, and now she remembered the whole silly conversation. He had quoted Shakespeare when he had advised her to sleep. Something else occurred to her. For the first time, she wondered how she happened to be in this particular spot. She glanced upwards, almost expecting to find the wreckage of the plane wedged in the midst of the pine tree, but she saw only the unfettered branches with their long needles. Was that the mark of the ponderosa?

"How did I get here?" she asked. "I couldn't have fallen in this spot."

"No, I brought you. It seemed like a good place—protected—though it was difficult to tell at night."

"You brought me . . . but you must have been hurt."

"I could hardly leave you in your seat." He shrugged.

Stacia swallowed and looked down. "That—that was good of you. I must have been heavy."

"No, not really," he said diffidently.

She continued to look down, studying her hands. She wished he had not played young Lochinvar or whatever—no, she could not wish that. She wished that she had not been so damned rude to him just now—but, she thought with a flare of anger, he had deserved it. If he had checked the plane out, they would have been in Las Vegas and he would be trading jokes with his best man, while she could be collecting some of those sights and sensations his mother feared to see in pictures and print. Still, he did merit at least a "thank you." Gruffly, she said, "I'm glad you didn't leave me in the plane. I guess I was . . . I mean, just now—"

"It doesn't matter," he said curtly, evidently anticipating and rejecting her apology. "Please, let's not go in for recriminations, etcetera, Miss Marshall."

She didn't like his tone. "That's okay with me," she said flippantly.

"Good. I'm glad we understand each other."

"Ditto," she said.

You always like to have the last word, don't you, Stacia? That was one of George's remarks. Under some circumstances, the answer was a definite yes. Paul Curtis was one of those circumstances, and she could only hope that Curtis Motors would fill the skies with planes, so that she would not need to remain in his company any longer than necessary! She could not imagine anything worse than that! No, on second thought, she could. George's company would have been worse—he would have left her in the plane.

chapter

3

STACIA ACHED ALL over. The mattress was hard, damned hard. George had always liked a firm mattress. "Great for your back," he had said enthusiastically. He was extremely concerned with matters of health—vitamins, he carried an arsenal of them! She moved restlessly. This mattress was the hardest yet! Why had they stopped at this motel? It was a ghastly place, with its huge red neon sign, "Open All Night," blinking on and off. Most couples who stopped here came only for a few hours. She had not wanted to check into it, but as usual, George was short of money, and they needed to break their drive across country somewhere. They were both short of money. He had been so angry, because she had refused to use her VISA card. He had been even angrier when she reminded him that it was so near its fifteen-hundred-dollar limit because he had charged so many expensive meals on it. "Filled up..." she muttered angrily. "It's all filled up, Georgie." He had never liked her to call him Georgie. It was undignified, he had complained. He had liked even less the other names she had called him at the last, when he had come to her with the news about marrying Marcella....

"Miss Marshall."

Who was calling her? Stacia moved restlessly and, putting her hand down, encountered pebbles. Pebbles!

22

How could there be pebbles in this bed? Bed? Consciousness was returning, and with it, understanding. Opening her eyes, she blinked against the bright sunshine. It aureoled the dark head of the man who stared down at her. To her surprise, he was carrying the small canvas tote that contained her makeup, her nightgown, terry-cloth robe and the dress which she would have worn while she was covering the wedding festivities. George, caught in her stream of consciousness, was washed down river. She was not lying on a hard, motel mattress but on the ground, which was not much harder. Above her was Mr. Paul Curtis, bridegroom in the wedding which, thanks to his carelessness, would not take place on this particular noon.

"I must have fallen asleep," she muttered.

"Yes, for two hours."

"Two hours!" She was displeased with herself. Falling asleep like that was giving in to weakness. Furthermore, it put her at a disadvantage as far as he was concerned. "I don't know how I happened to fall asleep," she said sulkily.

"Don't knock it," he returned. "You need sleep. You were badly shaken up."

"You were too," she growled accusingly.

"True. Fortunately, there were no bones broken, just assorted bruises. You're worse off. I don't know how your ankle got wrenched, but it's badly swollen. That's why I woke you up. You need to have your ankle strapped."

"Strapped?" she repeated, raising her eyebrows. "I guess an Ace bandage is required. We'll have to stop off at the nearest drugstore."

With a cold smile, he responded, "You do have a certain native wit, but we can do without a drugstore."

He patted the tote. "I was able to get this out of the plane. If you'll excuse me for examining the contents, I've found something I can use on your ankle." He held up a long white petticoat. "This is good, strong silk . . . or perhaps the dress?"

"Not the dress," she protested. "No." The dress in question represented practically the whole of a salary check from a special assignment. It had been more expensive than anything she had ever owned. It was more than a mere gown; it was a symbol. It stood for freedom. It was the first thing she had bought when she realized that George Lansing's marrying the rich Mrs. Marcella Griffin Bates came under the heading of a disguised blessing for Miss Stacia Marshall. It meant that her wages were strictly for her own use; she need never employ them to bail George out of some sticky financial situation and then wait until he paid her back out of one of his stock dividend checks, which were so long in coming. The dress was a creation from the designer floor at Lord & Taylor's. Of clinging jersey and amazingly packable, its lines were wonderful, and its color, a vivid green, matched her eyes. She had not yet worn it, and certainly she had not wanted to wear it at that damned wedding, not until she realized that George and his middle-aged bride would attend.

"I think we can make do with this slip, Miss Marshall," he assured her.

Stacia discerned a slight gleam in his dark eyes and interpreted it as amusement. She was immediately resentful. Was he teasing her because she had inadvertently displayed what, in her own mind, she did not hesitate to term an absurdly feminine streak of vanity? It did diminish her in strength. It might even cause him to believe that, despite the seriousness of their situation, she was exhibiting the silly, womanish traits that were probably common to the spoiled creatures he ran with. He must be shown that Stacia Marshall was not cut from that cloth! She considered giving a shrug but fortunately thought better of it, remembering the agony induced by other similar movements. She contented herself with saying airily, "Use either garment, Mr. Curtis; I couldn't care less." Something else occurred to her. "Only... isn't there a first aid kit on the plane?"

"There is. Unfortunately—"

"Someone forgot to stock it?"

"Bartlett, at the airport, was supposed to take care of that."

"And you didn't check it out?"

"I depended on him," he snapped.

"Oh."

"I didn't think anything'd happen. It's never happened before."

"Need I say—" she began.

"No, you needn't." He drew a long, hissing breath and expelled it in another hiss. "I've had the dubious pleasure of your company for only a short time and one we can reduce by however long you slept. However, I did get the flavor of your speech and I've read some of your articles. I know you have an admirable command of the language. I am sure you could spew out some choice phrases. Consider them said and duly recorded. And now let's strap that ankle." Reaching into his pocket, he brought out a large pocket knife.

The sight of it surprised Stacia. She hadn't expected to find him equipped with anything so useful. Quite as if he had read her thoughts, he added, "I carry this for sentimental reasons. It's a good thing, isn't it? Especially since it packs a scissors."

"Sentimental reasons?" she could not help questioning.

"Yes." He did not elucidate. Instead, he pulled out the minute scissors and made an incision in the material, ripping it down its length. He repeated the process until he had several long strips of silk. "We'll have enough for some changes of bandage," he remarked. "I'm going to bind your ankle now, Miss Marshall."

"All right," she said, tacitly giving him the permission he had not requested.

He knelt down slowly, carefully, his mouth a straight line, and a frown between his eyes. She guessed that he was hardly more comfortable than she. However, he was able to get around, which was more than she could do—thanks to him! Managing to get into a cross-legged position, he lifted her foot carefully and, placing it on his lap, unlaced the sneaker. She suppressed a little moan of pain as he eased her sock and shoe off. He was very gentle, she had to admit that, but her ankle was extremely tender. She did not like the looks of it—in addition to the swelling, it was darkly bruised.

"I know it hurts," he commented without looking up.

"I didn't say it hurt," she flared.

"I'm sure it does," he said positively. "I've had similar injuries. Anything wrong with a foot's a damned nuisance." He wound the strip of silk around her foot and ankle in what appeared to be a very professional manner. As he slit the end of the makeshift bandage and tied it, he said, "This might seem tight, and undoubtedly it will throb and smart, but it'll hold up better. Of course, you mustn't put much pressure on it. Fortunately, you're not very heavy."

For some reason, this observation made her feel even more diminished. She opened her mouth to assure him that, ankle or no ankle, she was not going to allow him to cast her in the role of "helpless female." However, she swallowed the retort. He had not been implying any such thing; he had been merely stating a fact. She was small and slender. She said gruffly, reluctantly, "It looks like a good job of bandaging."

"Um," he grunted. "When you're able to get about a little easier, you'll need to soak it in cold water. There's a stream down there." He jerked a hand over his shoulder. "That's lucky in several ways—at least we're not going to be thirsty."

She tensed. Inherent in his statement was an implication that could only cause her concern. Was he suggesting that they might be stuck here for more than a day or two? Her eyes fell on the neat rolls of bandages. He had spoken about *changes*. Changes? Was he thinking in terms of several days? How many days? A protest rose to her lips. She could not remain away that long. There was too much for her to do. There was her new assignment pending. Dave had promised! She made a face. Italy had been in the offing for some six months. It had taken some doing to persuade her editor to send her abroad—especially since she wanted to do an in-depth report on the Red Brigades.

"It's too dangerous," Dave had contended.

Stacia bit down a laugh. The wedding was not thought to be a "dangerous" assignment. Ha! Dave had not taken into consideration the Paul Curtises of this world—and their private planes! She turned her hot stare on her companion. "D—do you think—" she began, and paused, loathing the quaver she heard in her tone. He must not believe that she was afraid. She was not afraid; she was only concerned. She wanted to get on with her work. She loved it. It was exciting and rewarding. Above all, she did not want to be stuck up here—wherever here was—with a man she despised!

"Do I think what?" he prompted.

"They will search for you." Stacia turned her question into a statement, a positive statement, which, of course, it was. She had delivered it calmly. There had not been even a trace of anxiety in her tone—because she was *not* anxious. Thinking about it, she decided that there was no earthly way that the redoubtable Mrs. Curtis would let her only son and heir perish in the green vastness of the Sierra Nevada mountains. She was a lady with a well-established reputation for moving mountains, and she would move the whole range before she let that happen—provided, of course, that she knew they had landed in this area.

"Of course they will look for *us.*"

As before, he had emphasized the fact that there were two of them, something George would not have done. George had been great about minimizing her importance. Impatiently, Stacia drew a curtain over George. It was no time to think about him. "Will they know where to look for us? I mean, do they know what route you took?"

"I always take the same route, Miss Marshall—and yes, my mother's well aware of it. There's every reason to believe that rescue's on its way at this moment."

"When do you expect they'll get here?" she demanded.

"There's no predicting that," he said reasonably. "It could be hours or even days."

There was a pounding in her throat now. His mention of "days" had been a corroboration of her own fears, and he had spoken so calmly, so matter-of-factly! Why not? He didn't have any worries. He didn't have competitive colleagues like Randy Dobson, who might take over in his absence and prove that Stacia Marshall could be easily replaced—in all areas, because Randy could write as well as he shot pictures, and he had won prizes for his photography. Mr. Paul Curtis would get home, reschedule his wedding and live happily ever after, while she . . . She could imagine Dave being kind, conciliating and even regretful as he told her, "Well, honey, we had scheduled that Italian piece, and Randy . . ." Furiously, Stacia cried, "It can't take days."

"Unfortunately, these matters are beyond our control," he replied.

"God," she muttered between her teeth. "It passes all bounds of . . . of . . . I didn't want to cover this blasted wedding. I wanted—"

"And we didn't want you to cover it, as I think you know," he interrupted. "However, recriminations are useless. What happened, happened. Call it kismet. We're in one hell of a hole, and we've got to consider how we're going to get by until rescue does arrive. While you were asleep, I scouted around. I found a sort of crevice between two boulders where we can take shelter in case of rain."

"Rain? Oh, no, not that, too." She glowered at him.

He nodded. "Yes, I ordered it specially—because I knew we were going to crash."

"I suppose there were weather reports."

"A storm was predicted, but if we'd been able to keep on course, it wouldn't have rained until we arrived in Vegas. Unfortunately . . ." He glanced up at the sky.

She followed his gaze and saw that there were more clouds than there had been earlier. Some of them had a grayish tinge. They could get grayer, she thought bleakly. They could turn into thunderheads. She had been up in the Adirondacks during a rainstorm. The water had

come down in sheets. George had said that a nearby lake
had probably doubled in size. Their cabin had been very
cozy. There had been a big fur coverlet on the bed and
a roaring fire on the hearth and . . . She shied away from
that memory. She said, "What about the plane?"

"The plane?" he questioned.

"Couldn't we take shelter in it?"

"We couldn't chance it. The plane came to a stop near
a ravine. When I got your case out, it moved. There's
a chance it could go right off the cliff."

Stacia turned cold. "A ravine . . . we almost went into
a ravine?"

"Damn near," he replied grimly.

She could not restrain a shiver. Rather than lying
against the tree, she might have been smashed to pieces
on the jagged rocks. "Lord," she breathed.

"Don't think about it."

"I'm not," she flashed, hating anything that savored
of advice from Mr. Would-Be-Masterful-if-Given-Half-
a-Chance. Without a leg to stand on, he was the classic
male chauvinist pig. He was already trying to take command of the situation into which his errors had catapulted
them! Ankle or no ankle, he wasn't going to have that
opportunity. "You say you've looked around," she said.
"Have you any idea where we might be? You mentioned
something about ponderosa pines. . . ."

"I'm still not sure about our exact location in terms
of altitude. I've seen other types of trees around here
too. When I'm feeling a bit more fit, I'll be able to be
more informative. I'd say that by tomorrow, the muscle
strain should be easing. You'll probably feel more like
yourself too."

"I don't feel so bad now," she lied. "It's only my

ankle. I'm used to working under all sorts of conditions."

"The new woman," he murmured.

"Exactly!" she snapped.

"Good." He smiled.

She read mockery in his glance, mockery and something else. Could she term it anger? It occurred to her that Mr. Paul Curtis might have had quite a bit of experience with the "new woman." His mother might not be of that generation, but she, Stacia, certainly fitted into the mold.

She wondered about Gloria Mannon Meade. She had seen pictures of the bride. A slender, willowy woman, was she a reed, to bend before his mother? Quite possibly, since she had already been victimized by one Hamilton Harkness Meade, a man of impeccable social connections who had turned out to be a fortune-hunter. Gloria Mannon Meade had been much pitied. It was said that her husband had beaten her more than once. Stacia did not feel sorry for her. If any man had so much as raised a hand to her . . . but evidently, the lady of Paul's choice was not a fighter.

Was she even his choice? It was quite possible that his merger-minded mama might have engineered the wedding. Under the circumstances, Stacia wished that his mother had been piloting the plane. If she had, they would probably be toasting the happy couple by now. She . . . Her thoughts suddenly ceased. She had heard a noise, a faint buzzing noise. No, it was not a noise; it was a drone, a drone of motors, motors high overhead— a plane? Of course it was a plane! Unthinkingly, Stacia jumped up and started to run. She was conscious of an agonizing pain in her ankle, then not just in her ankle, but in her whole leg. She also heard a loud yell from

Paul Curtis. She had a glimpse of him rising swiftly and coming toward her; she felt his arm encircle her waist and then there was only darkness.

"Of all the damned idiotic things to do!"

Stacia stared at Paul Curtis with lackluster eyes. "I tell you I heard a—"

"Plane," he finished. Caustically, he added, "Can you possibly imagine that they could have seen us from that altitude and with all the trees around us and not even a signal fire?" He paused but did not give her a chance to answer as he continued accusingly, "You panicked, and that's something neither of us can afford to do."

She regarded him furiously. She was in no mood to endure his harangue. It was true that she had panicked, but under the circumstances, who would not have reacted as she had? She had heard the plane; she had not wanted it to zoom away without seeing her. Naturally, she had dashed toward that welcome sound, only to faint. More fury rose within her. She had never fainted in her whole life, and to have it happen in front of Mr. Ineffectual! That was not the worst of it. Fainting, she had discovered, was not merely a matter of blacking out. He had revived her by the age-old remedy of splashing cold water in her face—but when she awakened, she felt extremely nauseated—so nauseated that she had been unable to keep from throwing up! Paul Curtis had hurried away from her. Naturally, she had imagined him revolted by her action, but he had returned with water in the plastic top of some container he had found in the plane. He had made her wash her mouth out with the water and had gone back to the stream to bring her another cup—this time for drinking purposes. He had also brought a wet cloth and, despite her protests that she was able to care for herself, had insisted on wiping her face as if she were some helpless child! It was not compassion that had moved him; she was aware of that. He had only been trying once more to prove himself in command of their situation, which he was not and would never be, blast him. However, she had been placed at a definite disadvantage by that stupid faint. Thinking about it, her face grew hot. She blinked away tears of pure anger.

"Your ankle still hurts," he demanded, or rather, stated.

"I'm all right." She turned on him. "You spoke about signal fires. Don't you think it might have been wise to set one when you got up this morning? Then maybe that plane would have seen us."

"Oddly enough, I actually thought of that myself," he began, "but—"

"But you're given up smoking and you don't carry matches with you?"

"I always carry a cigarette lighter," he said, evenly but with an undercurrent of anger. "I don't smoke, but my fiancée does. However, Miss Marshall, had I used that lighter to start a fire, I might easily have set the whole mountainside ablaze. In case you hadn't noticed, it's June, and the grasses are dry.

Meeting his self-righteous glance, Stacia wondered if he expected an apology from her. He might expect it, but he'd better not hold his breath until he received it— he would turn blue. Maybe he did have a few grains of common sense, and if he'd used that same sense to check out the plane in the first place . . . but there was no use dwelling on that. He was right about one thing. It was ridiculous to indulge in recriminations. "If we can't start a fire, how are we going to be seen from the air?"

"When you're better able to get about, we'll have to

find some sort of rocky plateau where a fire can be built," he explained.

It occurred to her that he was a mountain climber. That was one plus in his favor—but even as that thought crossed her mind, she immediately knew just what sort of a mountain climber he must be—one who depended on pickaxes, clamps and ropes, on backpacks filled with supplies and, more important, upon an experienced guide. It was useless for her to even mention his climbing, she knew that, but still she could not help asking, "Do you have a rope?"

"A rope?" He stared at her quizzically. "Are you in need of a rope right now, Miss Marshall?"

"Not right now, Mr. Curtis. But I did think it might be helpful if we were forced to get down the mountain."

"You're quite right; it would have been helpful, but I do not have a rope. Fortunately, there are other methods of getting down mountains—which I will show you if it becomes necessary. However..." He broke off, frowning as a distant rumble resounded through the air.

Stacia stiffened. "Thunder."

"Thunder," he agreed regretfully.

She looked up at the sky and bit back a gasp of dismay. The clouds, which had been white with a grayish tinge, were now totally gray. They were also moving together—swirling through the sky like so many windborne ships. No, not ships; formless shapes, writhing about together—a nest of great gray slugs. She was both fascinated and repelled by that image.

He said, "I was afraid this might happen." He had been sitting beside her, but now he arose. "I am going to help you to your feet. I don't want you to put any weight on your ankle. Just balance on your good leg and then put your arms around my neck."

"What are you going to do?" she demanded.

"I am going to take you to that place I mentioned, before it starts raining."

"You don't need to carry me," she protested. "I can lean on you and hop."

"Dammit, will you stop arguing?" he said furiously. "I know you hate my guts, and maybe you have a point. As for me, I . . . well, I don't need to get descriptive. Of all the pigheaded, unreasonable . . . No, there isn't time to go into that." He spoke through gritted teeth. "It's going to rain cats and dogs. You don't want to add pneumonia to your list of injuries, because — you guessed it, Miss Marshall — I don't have any penicillin with me, either. Now, please try and cooperate. It's for your own damned good."

Some fifteen minutes later they were sitting next to each other in the space between two larger boulders and under the large slab of rock that turned the spot into a semicave. Stacia stared mutinously out at a rain so heavy it looked more like a silver curtain than a fall of drops.

She was leaning as far away from Paul as she could, given their restricted space. He sat with his back against the boulder on his side. Finally, he had stopped panting. A quick glance had shown her that his eyes were closed and that there were lines of pain on his forehead. Probably that was partially her fault. It had not been easy for him to carry her. She had tried to shift her weight as much as possible, but her hatred of being dependent on him had kept her from relaxing. She should have made more of an effort, but her resentment of him had grown so large that she could hardly bear touching him!

The situation could have been avoided so easily. If only he had taken a few simple precautions. Any other man would have done so, and without another thought —

but the rich Mr. Paul Curtis was used to delegating his responsibilities. Well, he had learned his lesson—but it was hardly fair that she should be a part of that learning process. She clenched her teeth. There were questions at the back of her mind, questions she wanted to avoid, but they were inexorably forcing their way into her consciousness, and there was no avoiding their prodding.

What was going to happen to them? It was raining very hard. How long would the rain last? How long would it be before they could move more easily—before her ankle healed? When would they be able to find a place where a fire could be lighted? When would the wood be dry enough that a flame might be kindled? What would happen if the planes flew over this area before they could prepare a bonfire? It was possible that the planes might not fly in this direction at all. Many things were possible, even probable. She did not want to think about them. She also did not want to think about the fact that she was cold and damp and altogether miserable. She shivered, and a flurry of little pains went through her.

"Miss Marshall..."

She started. "Yes?" she questioned edgily.

"Don't be a damned fool."

"What do you mean?" she demanded indignantly. Stacia tried to swivel about to face him but could not, because of the lack of space.

"Sit nearer to me. You need to keep warm, and so do I."

"I am warm."

"No, you're not." Shifting his position slightly, he put his arm around her waist. "Come, now," he urged. "Don't resist me. I don't like you any more than you like me, but I am sure that, in common with me, you do have the will to survive. Or am I wrong?"

"No," she admitted reluctantly, grudgingly, "you're not wrong."

"Ah, that's a real concession on your part." He spoke sarcastically. "Sit as close as possible, please," he instructed as she edged nearer to him. "I assure you that this is a survival technique and nothing more."

"You're damned right, it's nothing more," she muttered under her breath.

"I beg your pardon?"

"Nothing," she mumbled.

"Don't you feel more comfortable?" He drew her even closer into his embrace.

"Brrrr, you're cold," she said as the discovery struck her. "Your whole body."

"We'll both grow warmer soon. Now I have another suggestion for you. Try to sleep. That's also a survival technique."

Strangely enough within moments only, she was feeling much warmer. She expected that she would be able to sleep soon, and a random thought suddenly struck her. She could not conceal the laughter that shook her.

"You're still shivering," he said.

"I expect it'll stop soon." She could not have explained her laughter. She could not have told him that it had suddenly occurred to her that rather than covering Mr. Paul Curtis's wedding, she was, in a crazy way, covering the man himself. It also occurred to her that there might be an even bigger story to be written—once they got down the mountain. And then . . . off to Italy— with Rome the first stop! On that felicitous note, she fell asleep.

chapter

4

THE STREAM LAY between high banks heavy with foliage. It gushed over rocks, some smooth and others deeply ridged by the action of the waters. The larger rocks were dark gray under those rays of the sun that managed to penetrate the leafy vastness of overhanging tree branches. The smaller ones and the pebbles gleamed in shades of pink and yellow.

Stacia, her swollen ankle bare and soaking in those chill waters, was in no mood to appreciate the sylvan beauties about her. Two nights and most of a morning in the wilderness had wrought greatly on her nerves. Paul, now exploring their surroundings, had assured her that they were probably within reach of one or another trail in an area that was pretty well mapped. Under the circumstances, it was difficult for her to believe him. It was so quiet here—so remote. The trees grew densely about them; they could have been in some primeval forest at the beginning of time, she thought gloomily. She released a deep sigh. It was followed by an even deeper sigh as she contemplated her ankle, respository of nearly all her present woes.

"If only the damned thing hadn't been wrenched," she muttered for perhaps the thousandth time. It was amazing, the amount of difficulty it was causing. The pain was the very least of it. Because of her ankle, she was dependent on the man who had carried her down the bank and ordered her to soak it in the cold waters of this stream. It was dreadful to be so incapacitated. It put her at an extreme disadvantage and gave her companion an inflated sense of his own mastery.

He did not need any more inflating, she thought angrily. He had assumed control of their situation as easily as he had wrecked the plane. To a woman whose middle name should have been Independence, her situation was particularly galling. Resentfully, she stared at the trees, or rather, at the path he had taken through those same trees after he had left her. He had been gone quite a while, and where had he wandered? He had muttered something about trying to get a fix on their location, and also about finding some edible plants.

Food. Stacia had not eaten for a day and a half—and she had lost the supper she had consumed before takeoff, yet she did not remember feeling hungry yesterday. This morning was an entirely different matter. She was ravenous! However, she was also wary.

He could so easily poison her—by picking the wrong berries or grasses or whatever. Or would they be the wrong ones? He might be in the mood to get rid of her. She had been far from pleasant, and she knew he was angry. If she could give him credit for anything, it might be forebearance. He had commented very little on her attitude. However, even that served to irritate her. It suggested that he was used to being henpecked and had decided years ago that silence was the best defense. Or was he merely indifferent? And why did she need to spend so much time thinking about him? Again—because her ankle had turned her from a self-sufficient woman into something perilously close to his chattel. It had also forced her into an intimacy she loathed. She had not only slept near him the previous afternoon—she had remained with him that night, pressed so close against him that she could hear the pounding of his heart beneath her ear. However, much as she resented their closeness, she could not deny that the warmth had been welcome. To do him justice, he had not tried to take advantage of their enforced closeness. He had been marvelously impersonal.

Stacia laughed. Of course, he had been impersonal— he did not like her any more than she liked him. That was good. That was just the way she wanted it. Otherwise, her position would have been—and would be— extremely difficult. And where was he? He had been gone a very long time. She glanced at her watch and frowned. Against her will, she was worried about him. He had been away nearly two hours. Two hours!

She took her foot out of the stream. It was white, and the skin was crinkled from that long immersion. It felt numb, and had the swelling gone down? Not much. Experimentally, she pressed it and winced. It hurt. Nervously, she regarded the steep banks. It would be difficult getting up them, and what had happened to him? Could he have fallen off something—a cliff? So many mishaps could take place out here, especially to anyone unfamiliar with the terrain. There were animals, too...bears and deer and probably rattlesnakes. Where was he? There was a pulsing in her throat. Much as she did not want to see him, she wished he would hurry back.

"Miss Marshall."

She glanced up hastily, but did not see him. "Where are you?" she demanded edgily, expelling a breath she had not known she was holding.

"Here." He strode through the trees, to stand at the top of the incline. "Does your ankle feel better?"

"It should. I've been soaking it for practically two hours," she replied pointedly.

"Two hours!" He consulted his watch. "I didn't realize I'd been gone such a long time."

"Obviously," she snapped.

To her surprise, he laughed. "You really do have a miserable disposition. I shouldn't tell you my good news."

"Good news?" she echoed, and was annoyed with herself for the eagerness that sounded in her voice. "You—you've seen a plane?"

"Not a plane, but I've scouted out the area. I don't think we're far from the foothills. If worse comes to worst and they don't find us, I think we can get down to a trail. Your ankle ought to be stronger in another week or so, and—"

"Another week or so!" she repeated in horror.

"I don't say it'll be healed," he continued, evidently unaware of her shock. "But you might be able to put a little weight on it, and if we take it easy—"

"But a week. How can we exist up here?"

"It'll be possible. However, I don't say we'll need to exist up here that long. I've found a slab of rock where we can build our signal fire. I've also found a cave, which is larger than the one we shared last night." He gave her a brief ironic smile. "I guess you'll be glad of that."

She flushed. "Yes," she said shortly.

He climbed down the bank. "I'll take you there pretty soon." Pushing some leaves together, he stretched out on them with a long sigh. "I just need to rest a bit."

She thought he was looking a little pale. He had groaned more than once during the night. Hesitantly, she said, "Are you still in pain?"

He propped himself up on one elbow, his eyes wide. "Please don't." He laughed.

"Don't what?"

"Step out of character. You'll confuse me."

She glared at him. "I suppose you think you're being clever."

"Ah, that's better," he said, and shot her a grin of approval.

"If it weren't for—" she began hotly.

"My fetching you in the plane and letting my mechanic check it out as he always has before, rather than standing over him with an oil-can in one hand and a monkey wrench aimed at his head in the other to see that he did his work well, we wouldn't be in this mess. You see, I've paid close attention to all you've said. And now, please, could we have a ban, temporary at least, on the subject? I don't ask that we cement a lifelong friendship—that would be too much to expect—but I *do* think a little civility would be in order."

So many words were jumbled on Stacia's tongue that, for a moment, she was unable to utter any of them. That was indicative of her confusion. Thus challenged, she longed to reply that he hadn't deserved any better treatment than she'd accorded him. On the other hand, though, no matter who was responsible for their present situation, they might have to stay together for several more days. She did not rule out the week he had mentioned. Something else occurred to her. She had wanted to write an account of her experiences with the rich Mr. Curtis. In order to do that, she ought to know something about him. Sustained hostility would certainly stand in the way of insight. With all that in mind, she reached a decision. She would treat him as she treated all those she interviewed—in a distant but not unfriendly manner. In other words, her attitude would be strictly professional.

It was with her most professional smile, then, that she said, "You do have a point, Mr. Curtis."

"Bravo, Miss Marshall!" His dark eyes glinted with an amusement she immediately resented. Was he making fun of her? She opened her mouth and closed it. The comment that had trembled on her lips could never have been classified as professional. His gaze shifted from her to the stream. "Ah!" Plunging his hand into the water, he grabbed up some small leafy plants. "Cress, as I live and breathe!"

"Are you sure?" she asked dubiously.

He bit off a leaf. "Positive." He thrust the bunch at her. "Have some."

She hesitated. "But you ought to eat—"

"Please," he interrupted. "There's more where that came from. Look. It's all over the place. I wish I'd seen it before I left. I could have told you about it. You must be damned hungry."

She shook her head. "Not very." She thrust a few leaves into her mouth, thinking privately that she had never tasted anything half so delicious. "It's good," she admitted.

"Good?" His laughter set up a chain of echoes. "It's better than good. It's nectar and ambrosia." He ran his finger through the water. "The food of the gods in God's country. It's beautiful here."

"Beautiful?"

"The trees, the steams, the sky, the air. You're probably in no mood to appreciate it. Are you a city person?"

"I was born in New York."

"And love it, I expect?"

"Yes."

"Why are you here?"

She smothered a smile. He was interviewing her, but it was a way to turn the tables. *"Eyeview* has a Western office, as you know. I came her to write for the California edition."

"Temporarily, or on a permanent basis?"

"Temporarily. I was . . . I am due to go back at the end of the month." She had an interior wince, remembering the reasons she had come. It had taken longer than she had expected—for love to turn into hate. Fortunately, George had possessed enough bad qualities to tip the scale—but even so, it had been awhile before. she had gotten out of the habit of loving him. It was only a habit, she thought defiantly—and she had had enough of a change of scenery. She longed for New York.

"You'll go back at the end of the month, don't worry," he said.

"What?" Stacia looked at him blankly and then remembered her decision about a switch in her behavior and attitude. "Oh, yes, I'm sure of that. I mean . . . I'm not really frightened."

"Good." He gave her an approving look. "There really isn't any reason to be frightened. One way or another, we'll make it down the mountain."

He did have a positive approach. One had to admire that about him. By this time, George would have been a worse wreck than the plane! "I'm sure we will."

He was silent a moment as he grabbed another handful of watercress and munched it. "I was never much of a salad man," he said finally, "but I can't fault the cuisine. Have some more. Later, I'll supplement our diet. How does snake steak sound to you?"

She had been in the act of thrusting more cress into

her mouth. She coughed. "Oh, heavens, I hope you're joking."

"I am," he soothed. "Though rattlesnake meat does taste like chicken."

"Please," she begged.

"If you were back in New York, you'd probably think it was a great delicacy—along with chocolate-covered bees. Do you live in the city proper or out on the island?"

Stacia clutched at the change of subject like a drowning woman grabbing a life preserver.

"I'm on Sixty-first street just off Second Avenue. That's on the east side of town."

"I know. I used to live around there myself."

"You did?"

"Reasonably near. Fifty-fourth and First. It's a good place for a writer. It's a mad city, New York, but it breathes."

"Oh, it does," she agreed on a note of surprise. She had had him pegged as a strictly Western product. "You like it, then?"

He looked beyond her. "There was a time when I planned to settle there permanently."

"Really? But your plant's based in Nevada."

"My father was born in upstate New York. He came out to Nevada for his health."

"And prospered." She was becoming extremely interested. Without half trying, she was getting material for her article. She was thankful for the well-trained memory that Dave Lynch had compared to a tape-recorder, which she never took to interviews.

"Tape throws people," she had told him once. "They open up more easily if they don't believe it's posterity time."

"Dad prospered and died, too young, Miss Marshall.

He was only forty-four."

"That young!"

He nodded. "He worked too hard. He was a great man, a farseeing man, an understanding man, but it's not a good idea to get absorbed by a company. A business ought be a livelihood. It shouldn't absorb the life out of you like a fly in a spiderweb."

Stacia felt a twinge of contempt. It was the age-old story of the ant and the sluggard, and the sluggard was defending his way of life, as opposed to the work that had made it possible for him to enjoy his idleness. "I understand that Curtis Motors has a very good product," she said.

"Sure, it's a great product," he agreed, "but the pen is mightier than the Diesel engine."

"The pen?" she repeated uncertainly.

"Sorry, that's an in joke." He rose. "Your elephant is ready to bear you up the incline, or maybe your definition'd be different—such as an ass?"

She could not restrain a laugh. "I never gave you any such definition."

"You have the most speaking eyes, and it's been said that the eyes are the windows of the soul. I've achieved one victory with you, though. I didn't think it was possible."

"You didn't think *what* was possible?"

"I've made you smile."

Before she could think of a good retort, he had lifted her in his arms and was carrying her up the bank. With some concern, Stacia noted that his face had grown paler and his mouth was set in a rather grim line, as if he were biting back pain. "You can put me down," she said as they reached level ground. "I can hop."

"No—need—for—that," he replied, panting. "It's not—much farther."

In a few more moments, he brought her into a small clearing near the rocky face of a cliff. Cut into it was a cave, and at the entrance, she saw leaves and grasses heaped into a thick matting. He deposited her gently upon them and sat down beside her, his chest heaving with the exertion. His shirt was gaping open, and Stacia saw a gash just below his left nipple. A trickle of blood was running down his chest. "How did you do that?" she demanded.

"I've told you, you're not heavy."

"I don't mean me. Your chest's hurt."

He gave it a fleeting glance. "Oh, that. Nothing. I came into brief contact with a sharp twig this morning."

"It's bleeding."

"Is it?" He looked surprised. Glancing down, he said casually, "So it is. I thought it had stopped."

"It must have opened up again when you carried me—and why didn't you wash it when we were down by the stream?"

"It's nothing." He shrugged.

"It doesn't look like nothing."

"I've had worse scratches, I assure you—so you don't need to put on your Florence Nightingale cap."

To her surprise, she found that his eyes were sparkling with anger. Stacia felt snubbed and even a little hurt, but her curiosity was stronger than either of these two feelings. It was an odd reaction, she thought.

"Sorry," he added. "I didn't mean to bite your head off. It's just that . . . hell, it's nothing."

"Okay, I get the point—also the taste."

"The taste?"

"Of my own medicine." She laughed.

His laughter echoed hers. "I like that. On two counts. You're a better sport than I thought, and the product does come equipped with a sense of humor."

"The product used to have a very good sense of humor." Stacia sighed.

"And along came Harry?"

"Harry?"

"Or John or Bill or Dick or Clarence, somebody who upset your equilibrium and gave you a prejudice against all men?"

"Nonsense!" she said tartly.

"I'm wrong?"

"Yes!" she retorted.

"Do you know," he mused, "I don't believe that. I see petals beneath the prickles. Have you ever seen a cactus rose?"

"If you mean—" she began crossly.

He raised his hand. "Enough said, Miss Marshall. I promised you something to eat, earlier this morning. I've visited our larder." He made a sweeping gesture that took in the entire area. "And I have emerged with food."

"Food?" she said dubiously. "Not—"

"No," he assured her. "It's scaly but not serpentine." Rising, he moved farther back into the cave and came out holding a good-sized trout by the gills.

She stared at it in amazement. "How—I mean, without a line—"

"I tickled it," he said.

The explanation struck a distant chord in her memory, but at present she could not furnish a definition for herself.

"It couldn't stop laughing, and that's how I caught it," he explained.

He had a habit of making outrageous statements with a perfectly straight face; she remembered that from his mention of snake steak. It was a method of teasing her father had also used. She rather liked that about him. Thinking of her father, she remembered something else. "Tickling trout... You put your hands in the stream and hold them perfectly still and wait until a fish swims in and then you clamp down on them?"

"A few paces back from the head of the class, Miss Marshall, but something like that."

"I do know it takes a lot of patience."

He smiled at her. "I have a lot of patience. I never travel without it."

She flushed. "I'm glad." She looked away from him. "It must particularly have come in handy so far on this trip."

"Better and better, Miss Marshall," he said approvingly. "Pretty soon I shall insist that we be on a first-name basis."

She laughed. "I've no objection to that, Mr. Curtis."

"Paul."

"Paul... I'm Stacia."

"Stacia? Was it Anastasia, like the Russian princess?"

"No, it's Stacia after my great-aunt Stacia, whose mother was also a Stacia. It's a family name."

"Paul is also a family name. We trace it back to the saint. It's a great responsibility."

"You are mad!" she exclaimed.

"I try to be. It's the one way of keeping sane in this troubled world, Stacia."

"That's very profound, Paul."

"It would be more profound if we were both drunk," he told her solemnly. "But talking about drunk, Ebenezer, here, is waiting. I am going to make a fire and cook him. I wish he were a little larger, but—"

"The bigger one got away?"

"Ah, Stacia, you have a large fund of right answers."

She watched with some interest as he set about building a fire. He worked quickly and efficiently, piling up grasses, twigs, and small branches. From the depths of the cave, he had produced a slab of metal, evidently salvaged from the plane, and on this, he placed the trout. Putting the slab on top of the pile, he produced his lighter and set the wood ablaze.

Moving back, he said, "Thank you."

"For what?"

"For not asking me all sorts of questions while I was working. It's the sort of restraint I admire. Or are you an old hand at this sort of thing?"

"No, and I *was* curious. Where did you learn how to catch trout with your hands?"

His face softened. "From a man of whom I was very fond, Edward Grey. He was a neighbor of ours—meaning he lived about five miles down the road. After Dad died, he used to take me camping. It was he who got me interested in mountain climbing. He taught me a lot."

"He had a good pupil."

"Don't reform too much, Stacia; I won't know where I'm at."

"I expect I have been a bit—"

"Never apologize," he interrupted. "If that's what you had in mind. I could see your side of the situation. It was a very bad shock and you were hurt...incapacitated. I'd like to bet that's a new experience for you."

"Yes," she acknowledged ruefully. "But—"

"Shhhh," he sniffed. "Ebenezer has the floor. He's just told me that it doesn't take long to cook a fish's goose." He moved away from her, and a moment later,

he was back with the fish on the slab of metal. This he
held with a grease-stained rag, which, she guessed, was
also from the plane. Putting it on the ground between
them, he opened the trout and cut it into pieces. "Be
careful," he cautioned. "As they say at your favorite
French restaurant, 'ees a verry 'ot plate, mademoiselle.'
Especially since we don't have forks. And beware the
bones."

She smiled at him, "Yes, sir."

"I'm only telling you this for your own good," he said
defensively.

She had another smile for that. The smell of the fish
had reminded her that she was starving. Yet, she realized
ruefully, she dared not eat too much—certainly not all
of the half portion he was now pushing in her direction.
He must be even more hungry than she was—he had
been doing all the work. Four mouthfuls later, she said,
"That was heavenly, but I can't eat another bite."

He regarded her with surprise. "Yes, you can. I count
five more bites at least—six, if you take small ones."

"You have it."

"Don't be silly or self-sacrificing."

"Self-sacrificing!" She was stung by the truth. "I haven't reformed that much," she told him tartly. "I know
my own capacity, that's all."

"Must I force-feed you, Stacia? I know what you're
thinking, and it's very noble, but there's a forest of food
out there, which I intend to collect later, after I've built
the signal fire. Furthermore, one of the rules of survival
is that you eat." He tapped the metal. "Eat," he commanded.

"You and your rules," she grumbled.

"Eat," he repeated, a dangerous sparkle in his eye.
His hand strayed toward the fish. "I wasn't kidding,

Stacia. Eat the rest of your portion or I shall see to it that you do."

Her chin went up. "I dare you!" she challenged.

She had never seen anyone move so amazingly fast. In the twinkling of an eye, one of his hands was was under her chin and the other was propping her mouth open and pushing in the fish, several bites' worth. Laughter threaded the tone in which he commanded, "Swallow but don't choke."

The fish had landed in a part of her mouth that seemed to function independently of will. She could only swallow. The operation complete, she glared at him. "It was for your own good. I wasn't being noble or self-sacrificing. Unfortunately, I am dependent on you for my survival—and if you don't have enough nourishment, what's going to happen to *me?*"

He laughed heartily. "Ah, I like that. That is definitely in character. Consistency is a virtue, but since you are concerned about your welfare—let me assure you that we will both have enough of that 'nourishment' you're concerned about. I am only getting into my stride now, and with you to goad me, who knows what culinary marvels I may accomplish? What do you say to wolverine Provençale?"

"You do talk the most utter nonsense." She sniffed, but something strange was happening to the corners of her mouth. Despite his high-handed treatment of her, she could not help grinning. She liked his sense of humor. Amazingly enough, she was beginning to like *him*.

He smiled down at her. "A cactus rose, yes, indeed!" He quickly vanished into the depths of the cave and came out with a roll of silk in his hand. "I'm going to bind your ankle and then I'll set about building our signal fire."

"Don't you think you ought to rest?"

"Afterwards."

"But . . ."

He glanced up at the sky. "By my calculations, this portion of the 'wide blue yonder' ought to be filled with rescue planes, and soon. The rain kept them away yesterday, and that would make my mother all the more anxious. The fact that we haven't seen any suggests to me that they are combing other areas. They might arrive here at any time. Of course, I could be wrong, but in the event that I am not . . ." He knelt down, a movement he accomplished with more ease than he had the previous day. Inserting his knife in the knot above Stacia's ankle, he slit it open and unrolled the bandage. As before, his fingers were gentle as they probed the swollen flesh. "Does it hurt as much as it did yesterday?" he asked.

Earlier today, she would have insisted that it was much, much better. Of course, that would not have been the truth, but she wouldn't have wanted him to believe she was so dependent on him. Oddly, she was less eager to prove that point now. Besides, she knew him a little better than she had yesterday, knew him well enough to realize that she would have proved nothing, and certainly it was pleasanter not to be at odds with him. She said, "It's not quite as sore, but it aches. However, I think the soaking has helped."

"I think it has," he agreed. "It seems a little less puffy."

"Of course," she added, "some doctors think it strengthens strained limbs to walk on them."

"The profession is not without its sadists. As your medical adviser, I suggest you wait a few more days. By that time, you might be back in San Francisco—soaking it in Epsom salts in the privacy of your own bathroom."

She could not restrain a heartfelt, "Dear God, I hope so!"

"Think positively." He smiled. The binding of her ankle finished, he set about gathering wood.

Again, he worked efficiently—but more slowly, she thought, than when he had been preparing the fish. Watching him, Stacia feared he was doing too much. She wanted to object and to urge him to rest, but he had already made himself perfectly clear to her on that point. He seemed to resent any suggestion that he was not constructed from iron or steel. Recalling his flash of anger when she had mentioned the wound on his chest, she wondered about it. In spite of their growing friendliness, she still did not understand him. Indeed, how could she?—understanding of anyone did not come in two days, scarcely even in a lifetime. She shook her head, remembering her initial and instant estimate of his character. It did not begin to approximate him. It had been founded partially, if not wholly, on her own prejudices. He belonged to a stratum of society she had learned to dislike. Pace-setters, jet-setters—she had lumped them all together and entitled them, collectively, the insect kingdom. Grasshoppers and mayflies. The kingdom had been peopled by men such as George and women such as the pampered widow he'd wed. Paul Curtis did not conform to type.

"There," he said with some satisfaction.

Looking up, she saw him pointing to a large pile of wood. "Oh, that's great. That ought to burn for quite a while."

"I hope so. Still"—he laughed shortly—"we might be no more than a mile or so from a trail or even a camp."

"Do you think that's possible?" she asked dubiously.

"It's possible." He made one of his sweeping gestures.

"Here it looks as though we're in virgin territory, but territories, like women, are seldom virgin these days." He grinned at her.

She was intensely curious about that remark. "Do you regret the change in moral standards?"

"Only when it comes to land." In a moment, his smile vanished. "So much of it is poisoned, gutted, pillaged, drained."

"Yes." With a sudden flash of insight, she asked, "Is that why you like to climb mountains?" Before he could answer, she sighed. "I know the reply to that one. 'If I have to ask the question, I wouldn't understand the answer.'"

"I would never give you that hackneyed old response. There's a challenge about reaching the top. I like challenges and a change in perspective. You'd be surprised what can happen to you at the top of a mountain." He looked unexpectedly somber, but before she could probe further into his feelings on the subject, he had moved out of her range of vision, disappearing among the trees. He was back in a few minutes, his arms full of spongy-looking mosses, which, to her amazement, he spread on the pyre.

"Those look very damp," she commented. "Won't they keep the wood from burning?"

"They'll make the fire smoke—which is more visible at a distance than flames. Remember how the Indians of old used to communicate from peak to peak? Smoke by day—and flames by night, that's our objective."

"Would they come at night? The planes?"

"They might. The moon will be nearly full tonight." He laughed shortly. "You can thank Gloria for that."

"Gloria?"

"My fiancée." He cocked a derisive brow. "Surely

you've heard of her, Madame Reporter from *Eyeview?*"

"Oh, yes, yes, Gloria Ti—uh...Mannon Meade."
Stacia reddened, and was thankful that she had caught
herself in time.

"The same."

"And what does she have to do with regulating
moons?"

"She's into moonlight in Venice."

"That's right. You were going to spend your honeymoon in Venice."

"You have done your homework after all." He smiled.
"Yes, by now we should have been standing on the balcony of a storied palazzo hard by the Rialto Bridge,
seeing the moon reflected in the inky waters of the Grand
Canal and listening to the dulcet and possibly tenor tones
of a passing gondolier—all the trappings of high romance." He shrugged. "Still, a moon is a moon, wherever it shines, don't you agree?"

"Indubitably." She smiled, but her curiosity was once
more piqued. He had spoken as if, indeed, the romantic
trappings of that Venetian honeymoon amused rather than
excited him. Stacia recalled her earlier suspicion that his
marriage to Gloria Mannon Meade had been made in the
boardrooms of their parent companies. Had she been
correct? It was a strangely unwelcome thought. Paul
Curtis did not seem the type of man who would lend
himself to so cold-blooded a coupling. Yet, she realized,
twenty-four hours earlier, she would have found his cyn-
ical attitude entirely in keeping with her estimate of his
character. Twenty-four? She could narrow it down even
further, to as little as three. In three hours, her opinion
of him had changed almost completely. She liked him.
She even respected him, but she did not understand him,
and...she coughed as a gust of wind-driven smoke en-

tered her nostrils. Startled, she stared at the wood and found it ablaze.

Paul hastened back to her. "Come," he said. "I have to move you out of range of that smoke." Kneeling, he gathered her up in his arms and took her closer to the entrance of the cave. As he put her down, he said, "The wind is blowing in the other direction, so you shouldn't be bothered by the smoke here."

She looked at the tall column of smoke. "You were right about the mosses."

He nodded, saying with pardonable satisfaction, "It *is* a good fire. It should get us off the mountain."

"It certainly should, and—" Stacia broke off, wondering if she was actually hearing a distant drone—the drone of a low-flying plane! "Is—is it possible?" She looked at Paul and found him cocking his head and staring into the distance.

He turned back toward her, his eyes bright with excitement. "Yes, it is a plane. How's that for timing?"

"Incredible!" Stacia cried. Yet, to her utter surprise, she found that she was not as excited as she had imagined she would be. It was very confusing. Her eyes lit on Paul Curtis and she realized with a painful twinge that it was not as confusing as all that. The end of an association she had begun to enjoy was now in sight—very much in sight, she realized as she saw the sunlight reflected on the silver sides of the approaching plane. Was it searching for them? Or would it pass out of sight, as the other had?

Her question was answered as it circled the area, came back and circled again, dropping lower. She did not need Paul's joyful assurance, "Rescue's at hand, Stacia." It was very evident to her that the pilot had sighted the column of smoke.

With some hasty rescheduling, Gloria Mannon Meade had every chance of enjoying that full moon in Venice after all, and she, Stacia Marshall, would have an exclusive on the groom that no other magazine in the world could match. Well, at least Dave Lynch would be pleased, she reasoned, and fixed her eyes on the circling plane.

chapter

5

"IT'S MIRACULOUS," PAUL SAID.

He was standing several feet away from Stacia on the other side of the fire. She saw his tall figure through the smoke. It looked wavering and insubstantial—an effect she wished she might have captured on film. She had a pang of regret for her smashed camera and the other delicate equipment lost in the crash. Her momentary regrets quickly vanished. Her reporter's eye took over, savoring the drama of imminent rescue. Sentences spun through her head. She knew exactly how she would describe the small, graceful plane as it swooped about the area—and then she coughed as once more gusts of smoke blew in her direction. The wind had changed, and it had also grown much stronger. Eyes smarting, she pushed herself as far away from the smoke as possible, and in that moment, she heard a hoarse shout from Paul.

"No, oh, no, for God's sake, man, that's too far. Pull out of it. Christ!"

"What is it?" Stacia called, turning toward him.

"A downdraft. He's caught in a damned downdraft...the wind..."

Out of smoke-blurred eyes, Stacia stared ahead and saw a flash of silver in the distance. It was accompanied by a whistling roar, and then there was a shattering, crunching sound that filled the air briefly and died away into the silence. Sound tore out of her own throat, too. She was hardly aware of it, hardly aware of her long, horrified screams.

"Stacia, don't." Paul was back at her side, coughing. "Oh, God, the smoke. Here, let me get you away." He scooped her up in his arms and carried her down among the trees, away from the place where, in the distance, another spiral of smoke rose black against the horizon.

Stacia was hardly aware of being put down on a patch of grass, of being gathered into Paul's arms, of his half-inarticulate murmurs as he stroked her hair. Though she was not given to tears, she could not stop crying. The suddenness of the accident had been more than she could bear. Once more she was Stacia Marshall, aged nineteen, hearing the incredible news that her parents were not coming home, seeing, in her mind's eye, the huge plane crashing into the sea. It was too much. "Mother . . . Daddy," she moaned, trying to gather herself together, trying to stop crying, but the tears squeezed themselves between the guarding eyelids and ran down her cheeks. "The p—poor pilot," she said, weeping. "The s—same way . . . dead, all dead . . . the same way." Her sobbing turned into dry hiccoughs, through which she heard Paul's comforting assurances. There was comfort, too, in his sheltering arms.

At length, Stacia pulled away. Her wild grief had subsided. She felt drained, weak . . . and terribly embarrassed. She was not a weeper. The agony over the death of her parents had been a grief endured in silence. Alone and dry-eyed at the memorial service, she had been dubbed hard and unfeeling by her parents' friends. "I—I'm sorry," she managed to say, not looking at Paul, looking instead at the ground, strewn with pine needles and small pebbles.

His hold had relaxed, but there was still gentleness

in his voice as he said, "Don't be sorry. It's understandable—and a damnable thing. The wind changed, and he must have been caught off guard."

"Looking for us," she answered with a moan.

"Yes," he agreed grimly. "It's not the first time an accident like this has occurred." Huskily, he added, "It's so damned useless. His life..." He broke off. "It's no good dwelling on it."

"No."

"Your parents," he said tentatively. "Was there an accident?"

Stacia nodded, looking at him now, seeing concern and sympathy in his gaze. "They went down in a plane, on the way back from Greece.

"Oh, God, I didn't know that."

"How would you?"

He regarded her curiously, then with surprise. "I wouldn't, would I?" he said slowly.

His remark was singularly revealing, Stacia thought. It was indicative of the closeness they had achieved without any real knowledge of each other. There were still so many gaps to be bridged, so many gaps that would probably never be bridged.

As if that idea had also occurred to him, he said, "When did it happen? Your parents' accident?"

"Six years ago."

"You couldn't have been very old."

"I was nineteen."

"That isn't very old. I'm sorry."

Oddly enough, his sympathy brought her tears near the surface again. She wondered at that. There had been numerous expressions of sympathy tendered to her at the memorial service. They had all seemed false. His did not. "Thank you," she murmured.

He shook his head. "And twice in three days to have

experienced something like it all over again. You've stood up remarkably well."

Stacia found it necessary to turn away from him again. In a muffled voice, she said, "How can you tell me such a thing? After just now . . ."

"Dear lady, you're not made of stone. Seeing his plane go down must have brought your parents' accident very vividly to mind—and there was your own recent brush with disaster, and even without any of that, witnessing a death is terrible."

"Yes, oh, yes," she breathed. "It was so *needless*. That's what I thought when my parents died. I was in college. They had this great opportunity for a second honeymoon. The Greek islands in the spring, all expenses paid, because my father was shooting."

"Shooting?"

"He was a photographer, a good one. My mother'd been a high-fashion model. That's how they met. He was a free-lancer. He had a lot of accounts. One of them was *Harper's Bazaar*. He photographed her in this wild dress and told her afterwards that with her hair piled on top of her head and all her bones showing, she looked like a starvation case. She was furious, but evidently it started her thinking, and she admitted that she agreed with him. They fell in love, and she learned how to cook and gained a lot of weight. They were so damned happy together. They never stopped being happy. She went around the apartment singing. God, she had the most t-t-terrible voice." Stacia swallowed and found she could not talk about them any more. Determinedly, she stared at the ground.

He slipped his arm around her again. "That's a really beautiful story."

"It ought to—to have had a h-happier ending," Stacia croaked.

"There was happiness while it lasted. That's something too. I bet a lot of people envied them that."

She nodded. "A lot of them tried to break it up."

"Par for the course," he said, "but they didn't succeed."

"They couldn't."

"That's good. That's damned good. And don't tell me that they never quarreled. I'm sure they did."

Stacia found she could laugh. "The most blazing rows."

"And that was good too. They got mad—but they found they could trust each other. That's one of the greatest things in the world, Stacia—being able to trust the person you love."

Something in his tone made her look sharply at him. She found that he was staring into the distance, a frown on his face. She wondered what memories she might have activated. She guessed that they were not happy, and without knowing why, she was sorry for him. Probably the key to that unhappiness was in his words about trusting. He must have been disappointed in someone. Also, it seemed to her that there had been a touch of envy when he had spoken about her parents. That was strange. He was on the very brink of marriage. One would think...but she recalled what she had thought, and very recently, about the marriage he was making with Gloria. She wished there were some way she could get to understand him better, but that was unlikely. A few barriers were down, but only a few.

He moved away from her and stood up. "We'd better go back up the hill. I'll need to pile more wood on the fire. Undoubtedly he will have radioed his position. Other planes will come. They might be here soon, and..." He hesitated, swallowing and blinking rather fast. "They might be confused by the smoke from his plane." He regarded her with concern. "Will you mind returning?"

"No," she assured him quickly. "I only wish I didn't need to be such a burden to you."

"How many times and in how many ways must I tell you that you are not a burden to me? Now, please, let's have no more of that foolish talk!"

"Yes, sir," she said meekly.

"That's better." Bending down, he lifted her with ease.

The wind had shifted yet again, and the smoke had diminished, but from the gully into which the plane had fallen, the black fumes from the burning wreck still streaked up into the sky. Stacia bit down the groan that threatened to escape from her, but Paul heard it. He said softly, "Don't look." His arms tightened about her briefly, and then he set her down before the mouth of the cave. "I'll tend to the fire," he added, the huskiness back in his voice again.

"Afterwards, you will please come and lie down," she said severely. "You're doing far too much."

"I—" he began, but stopped abruptly. His head lifted, his eyes were narrowed as he listened to the low rumble in the distance.

Stacia said incredulously, "That sounds like thunder."

"It's thunder, all right," was his laconic response.

Looking skyward, Stacia saw huge wind-driven clouds bent on blotting out the sun. "No," she protested. "Not again."

"Better move back into the cave," he advised.

She was glad he did not offer to lift or pull her. She could accomplish this necessary movement by herself, slithering and propelling herself with her hands toward the overhanging rock. Meanwhile, Paul was gathering the wood he had not used in building the fire. He dumped a load of it into the cave. He had just enough time to gather another armful before the clouds split and the rain pelted down again, quelling the flames of the signal fire and, to Stacia's unexpressed relief, dowsing those of the fallen plane as well.

Stacia, blinking against bright light coming into the cave, put out a tentative hand. She touched leaves, terry cloth and leather. The leaves were below her, and the rest on top to keep her warm, but the real warmth came from the man who lay close beside her, so close that she could feel the thudding of his heart. He was still deeply asleep, the lines of anxiety smoothed from his forehead and around his eyes. But she knew they would be back once he awakened. The dark stubble that coated his cheeks and chin did nothing to detract from his handsome features. In sleep, George had had a vacuous expression, but Paul's strength remained. Watching him, Stacia was filled with a mixture of regret, frustration and confusion—regret for the prejudices that had animated her when she had first met him.

If only they had encountered each other under different circumstances . . . but if she were to be realistic about it, they could not have encountered each other at all in different circumstances. The circles in which they moved were not concentric. If it had not been for her interview with the Sausa Seven, she would have been on the plane with her colleagues. She would have seen him from afar

and through prejudice-blinded eyes. She would have
written one of her mock-serious pieces about his wedding—cleverly damning the bride and groom. Or would
she have depicted the bride as a victim and the groom
as a predator? Possibly. At this point in time, she was
wondering about Gloria Mannon Meade, the unknown
quantity.

No, she was not entirely unknown. In addition to her
research on Mrs. Meade's unfortunate first marriage,
Stacia had discovered a little about her background. She
had emerged with information that, in her estimation,
categorized Gloria as the typical rich girl. She had been
to the best schools, she had dabbled in social work, had
married at twenty. After the ugly divorce, she had licked
her wounds in Sardinia before appearing with numerous
other eligible bachelors in posh spots around the world.
It had been two years since she had parted from her first
husband. The engagement to Paul Curtis had come as
a surprise—especially because the pair had known each
other most of their lives. A particularly cloying article,
ghost-written for Mrs. Meade and appearing in one of
the major women's magazines, had spoken about the
"sudden realization" which had overtaken them both. It
had described the "incandescent moment" when friendship had become love.

Did he love her?

Once more, Stacia cast her mind back to the photo-
graphs she had seen of the bride. Invariably, the accom-
panying captions had described her as the "beautiful"
Gloria Mannon Meade. Stacia disagreed with that. Her
mouth was too large, her jaw too long, and her nose was
long, too. Her eyes were her best feature—large and
dark. Her hair was as dark as Paul's, but without the
deep waves that rippled through his locks. She wondered

if Gloria's eyelashes were as long; they had looked long in her pictures, but they could have come from a box. Probably they had.

Stacia felt her cheeks grow warm. She was uncharacteristically hasty to find fault with Paul's fiancée, but she just could not see her as a victim any more. In fact, something told her that Mrs. Meade was not worthy of the man she was marrying. Not worthy? Stacia hastily swallowed a laugh. There had been a time when she had believed them ideally matched. That was B.C.—Before the Crash—before she had begun to know him, before she had started to ... She paused, her mind shrinking from that word, that four-letter word starting with "l" which still frightened her, and with reason—it was twice as dangerous to her peace of mind now ... more than twice.

Mentally, she weighed all the reasons against it. They were in an unnatural situation, an artificial situation. They had been thrown together not out of choice but by accident. She had put her worst foot forward and kicked him with it, verbally. He would not soon forget the stings she had inflicted. She had been totally unreasonable. She knew that now and wished this particular enlightenment had occured sooner.

"'If wishes were horses,'" he had said in answer to that first jibe, which she had not meant him to overhear; but, she remembered with a pang, she had not cared that he did.

Must she dwell on what had taken place between them in the beginning? They were friends now—friends, yes, but she wanted more. No use lying to herself; it was very hard to be so close to him, to have his arm cradling her and to know that he felt no stirring of desire for her. Was that entirely true? Yesterday ... but was she putting far too much emphasis upon something as minor as the incident which she had been remembering at odd intervals ever since it had happened?

Yesterday had been a long and difficult day. Difficult, frustrating and depressing. Their only consolation had been that the cave was warm. Paul had built a small fire near the opening. It had given off enough heat to fill what was a relatively small space, scarcely higher than his head when he was standing, and not much more than eleven or twelve feet deep. It had afforded protection from the rain. The rain! It had been heavy in the night and heavier in the morning. They had breakfasted on the wilted cresses Paul had brought back from the stream, and on some wild blackberries, which were good—but not very filling. They had wiled away some of the time with Twenty Questions and other games, but their interest had flagged, and they had fallen into silence as they watched the incessant rain. Stacia had finally fallen asleep, to be gently awakened by Paul at about one in the afternoon.

"It's stopped," he had told her. "I'm going to look for food."

A glance outside had shown Stacia that there was no sign of real clearing. The sky remained lowering, and the thunderheads were massing for another onslaught.

"It's going to rain again, and soon," she had told him worriedly.

"I'll have to chance it," he had insisted.

Now she felt a lump in her throat, remembering her fear when the rain had begun again before he returned. She had imagined him falling into the swollen stream and being borne down the mountain. She could hear the roaring of the waters in the distance. Had he dared to search for water cress there? No, he would not have been so foolish. Unlike George, he knew his way around the wild places of the world. Still, she had also imagined Paul slipping in the mud and rolling down a steep incline to—what? He had mentioned a ravine. It would be easy to make a misstep, especially in such a rainstorm! She had tried to console herself by remembering her earlier fears when she had awaited him by the stream. He had been gone over two hours then, but it had not been raining. Waiting in the cave, she had checked her watch, but then recalled that, since she had not looked at it when he left, she had no idea how long he'd been gone. She had been frantic by the time he returned, his arms full of grasses and ferns. And, of course, he was soaked to the skin.

Naturally, he had stripped off his clothing, putting it on a boulder close to the fire. His body, lithe, slender yet powerfully muscled, and bare save for his jockey shorts, was a golden tan, and largely free from hair. Fortunately, as a photographer, she was no stranger to the beauties of the masculine form. Yet Stacia had not expected to be so excited by the sight of Paul's body. It had been very, very difficult for her to sound calm and matter-of-fact when she said, "Best lie near me. It's not very warm in here."

He had not hesitated to avail himself of that invitation. Stretched out beside her, he had lain there silently, eyes shut, pressing against her—his arm loosely about her. Stacia drew a deep breath, remembering when that arm had tightened, when he had begun to breathe heavily. She had tensed, wanting him yet not wanting him, or rather, not wanting to be merely a warm, willing body. Had he felt her slight movemements? Had he interpreted it as fear, or had he experienced second thoughts of his own? She did not know, but he had moved away, not far, but far enough to spell withdrawal. Had she only imagined he had been aroused? Had it been merely a reflex? There was no knowing. The moment had passed, and he had fallen asleep.

He had awakened later to cook some of the roots and to serve others raw. They had been surprisingly palatable, and another batch of wild blackberries seemed even more delicious than they had that morning. However, at his warning, they had not eaten too much of anything. She smiled, remembering his unexpectedly hesitant references to the physical discomforts attendant upon putting too much unusual food into the system.

"You're probably speaking about that popular Mexican disorder called Montezuma's revenge." Stacia had hazarded with a laugh.

"Or the Pharaoh's curse, as it is known along the Nile." He had nodded and grinned back at her.

"You've been to Egypt?" she had asked.

"Briefly. On an assignment."

"An assignment?"

"I've done some travel writing," he had said deprecatingly. "Not much."

"Really?" She had been surprised and interested. "For what?"

"The Reno *Call;* it's an independent. A friend of mine owns it."

"Oh, I see." Thinking of that brief explanation and her own comment, Stacia wondered if he had heard the resentment in her tone. She had been resentful, remembering that connections counted for a lot in the writing game. If you knew somebody and could spell "cat," you could end up with an article assignment. A patient editor would do the dirty work, and your by-line would blossom above the finished product. Considering it, she was sure he had picked up on her thoughts—for he had given her a penetrating look and changed the subject.

Later in the day, he had grown moody, staring silently at the pelting rain, his brow knotted. Toward nightfall, he had told her what was on his mind. "We're not going to be able to stay up here any longer. There's a place where we could get down; I scouted it yesterday. I also think I've about figured out where the wreckage of that plane is. We've got to make it over there."

"Why?"

"Because when those search planes come back, they'll be able to see it from the air. The poor devil didn't have our luck. He fell on rocks. Unlike the Cub, his plane's not sunk in shrubbery. It will be much more visible. We'll need to build our fires in that vicinity. And there's a way to get to it. It's arduous but it's not dangerous, not if you're cautious. I could show you how to be cautious. It all depends on your ankle."

She had said quickly, "It's not hurting as much as it did. I could probably walk on it."

"You won't need to *walk* on it," he had replied, "but there are moments when you might need to put your weight on it, though not for long."

"What must I do?"

"It will be a matter of finding footholds."

"On what?"

"The cliffside. The wood's wet, you see."

"The wood? Shall we be walking on wet wood?" Stacia had demanded confusedly.

Paul had flushed. "I'm not making myself clear. I've got too much on my mind, I guess. It's this way. We won't be able to build another signal fire here. The wood's soaked through. We can't stay up here—eating this sort of fodder. As I said, we've got to make it to that wreckage—and the only way's to crawl down the cliff. It's a steep incline, but once you get the hang of it, you can manage. It's got one thing going for it. Most of the way, we won't be wet. There's a thick layer of tree branches above it. The only hazard will be the pine needles. You can slip and slide on them, but it'd take some doing to really injure yourself." He had hesitated before asking, "Are you game?"

"Of course." She prided herself on not having hesitated a second.

His eyes had lit up, and once more she had become aware of the golden flecks in them as he said, "You have a lot of courage, Stacia. I really admire that." He leaned over and kissed her lightly on the lips. Before she could think of a thing to say, he had added, "I suggest we get as much sleep as possible. We'll need it. And let's hope that by morning, it will have rained itself out."

"Let us pray," she had said lightly.

He had put a few more sticks of wood on the fire and slipped into his clothing. They had huddled together under his jacket and her robe. He had fallen asleep quickly, and finally, she had slept too. She winced, remembering the dream that had seemed to fill most of the night, though it probably had taken only a few moments, if that long. The length didn't matter—the content remained with her. It had seemed so real. She and Paul had been walking down a long, broad road, hand in hand. He had looked at her so lovingly, his brown eyes warm, as they had never been in all their time together here. He had whispered in her ear, "Damn it, Stacia, I'm falling in love with you."

She had been about to respond in kind, when she saw the girl standing before them, smiling and waving at him, beckoning to him. She had felt him draw away from her, and then he was running toward the other woman. Stacia had recognized her immediately. She looked just like her pictures. In fact, she seemed to be a photograph in black and white—Gloria Mannon Meade. The scene had changed, as scenes do in dreams, and Stacia had watched that photograph change into a woman with dark eyes, a woman in a bridal veil, sailing down the moonlit waters of a Venetian canal without benefit of gondola, but on the surface of the water, sailing away from her, wrapped in Paul's arms.

She didn't need any Freudian psychiatrist to furnish interpretations of that dream. It was her conscience telling her that she had no right to weave fantasies about a man who would have been on his honeymoon were it not for the malign fates. No matter how sneeringly he had described that Venetian scene, he would have married Gloria Mannon Meade. Knowing him, she did not believe he would have taken such a step lightly. He was not a man who could be pushed around. He did not need the Meade money. Consequently, there was only one reason why he would have agreed to marry Gloria—he must love her. Probably it was one of those things—they had been friends for such a long time, he had not divined his real feelings toward her until recently. And certainly, he was being faithful to her. Plenty of men in his present circumstances . . . Stacia flushed. It was utterly reprehensible of her to wish that he had taken advantage of the situation. She ought to respect his restraint. Intellectually, she respected it. It was only that being so close to him . . . She did not want to dwell on that, must not dwell on it.

Her dream might have been a warning, a warning from the depths of her unconscious mind to keep her distance and her cool. She must remember the swiftness with which he had parted from her and gone to the image of Gloria Mannon Meade. But the whisper...'why in hell did she have to keep thinking about that whisper? Because it had seemed so real. She could remember times when she had fallen asleep with the television tuned in to an old movie. The dialogue had worked its way into her dreams. What if...what if he had really spoken? Down, girl, she told herself sternly, you are definitely building castles out of sand!

She stared up at the roof of the cave, at the grayish rocks. It was not a very interesting cavern—no stalactites dripping from above and, fortunately, no stalagmites growing upwards from the floor. It was less a cave than a crevasse or fissure in the rocks—no, "cave" was the better description. She remembered her thoughts by the stream, about the beginning of time. They *were* cave dwellers, as their distant ancestors had been. In those days, she bet no questions had been asked as to the way of a man with a woman—she felt her cheeks grow warm again. Why was she so concentrated on that? It was not her habit to yearn for men who could never be interested in her, and quite truthfully, a great number of men were interested in her.

In the last seven months, there had been quite a few applicants for George's position in her life. However, none of them had measured up to George. Now George had paled to a mere ghost beside the vibrant personality of the man beside her. Furthermore, she was aware, and for the first time, that she had never really loved George. She had loved the concept she had of him. As for Paul...she had a moment of wishing she had never grown to respect him. It had been safer that way—or had she been attracted to him from the very first? Had her initial reaction been merely a defense mechanism? She sighed. It hardly mattered.

"Are you in pain, Stacia?" Paul murmured.

She started. "You're awake!" she exclaimed.

"Just. You sighed."

"I was only breathing deeply," she said quickly, turning to face him and regretting the withdrawal of his nearness as he sat up. "Did you sleep well?"

"Very well." He smiled, his eyes lingering on her face. "You look rested."

"I am," she told him, wondering if she were mistaken in thinking that there was a new warmth in his glance. A second later, she was sure she was wrong, as he added, "I see that the sun's up at last, thank God."

"Yes." She nodded. "We'll be able to go hiking, or climbing, as the case may be."

He said anxiously, "How's your ankle?"

"Much better. All this rest I've had has been good for it."

He regarded her steadily. "Are you sure?"

"Positive." With a little gurgle of laughter, she added, "I'm sure that I've proved I've got precious little in the way of the blood of the martyr."

"As I think I've told you, you have more than your share of courage, though. In fact, I find you—" He paused, and then added huskily, "—one of the most courageous women I have ever met."

Had he wanted to say something else? Stacia wondered, and was angry at herself for putting more sand bricks in the foundation of that castle. She said with a light laugh, "I hope you'll be of that same opinion once we've started down the incline."

"If I weren't sure it was relatively safe," Paul said

earnestly, "I would never let you start. I'll be right beside you, as close as is humanly possible. And remember, it can be done, though you might not believe me when you first see it."

"I trust your knowledge, Paul," she said firmly. "I'm not the least bit afraid."

"Thank you," he said. "I like you, Stacia. More than that, I admire you."

Stacia flushed. His tone was similar to the one she had heard in her dreams, but this was reality, with the sun shining on it. She found she could say quite steadily and without any of the disappointment she felt clouding her tone, "I like you, too, Paul—and it goes without saying that I admire you." She reached out her hand, and he clasped it warmly.

"Friends—good friends at last." He grinned.

chapter

6

FEELING LIKE A limpet as she pressed closely against the cliff face, Stacia descended slowly. It seemed to her that she had been there for hours. It was necessary to amend her limpet comparison, too. Limpets were organisms that could really stick to surfaces; they were made that way— small, round and flat. They were—she recalled a definition from Biology I—"gastropod mollusks who cling tightly to surfaces when disturbed."

She was disturbed—totally terrified would be the better description! Unfortunately, though, she lacked the ability to cling tightly. Furthermore, limpets did not need to back down, depending on bushes, shrubs and saplings to bear their weight as they groped with the feet they did not possess for a toehold in the shale, limiting their gaze to the length of their body alone—because their trusted companion and guide had told them that to look down too far would frighten them.

Remembering her initial introduction to that incline, Stacia controlled a reminiscent shiver with difficulty. It had seemed absolutely straight up and down, and for a moment, her newly acquired confidence in Paul had almost evaporated. No one could negotiate that perpendicular cliff without coming to harm! She was sure of it, but Paul had seemed so calm as he had indicated the clumps of greenery that would aid her descent.

"It's only a matter of finding what will bear your weight. Look for thick stalks. Stay away from withered woody stems. They are likely to break in your hand. Beware of saplings that bend too far. Notice how close the shrubs and bushes grow. They will be within easy reach. Grab one, pull at it and see how firmly anchored it is in the shale—then clutch it. Stay as close as possible to the side of the cliff; put your foot on these rocks that jut out from the soil. Generally, you don't need to look for a toehold. You can find it with your foot. Try to use your right foot as much as possible. If you should slip on the pine needles, your fall will be broken by bushes. I assure you that you shouldn't be afraid—not if you follow my directions."

"I'm not afraid, not in the least." Partly to reassure herself as well as Paul, she had continued, "You've no idea the places I've scaled in order to get a picture— ledges you wouldn't believe." That had been true. She had failed to mention that there had always been scaffolding, ropes and nets. They had given her courage, but, she reasoned, if she had fallen off the ledges, they would not have been of much use. And after all, this time she wouldn't be alone; Paul would be beside her. "I'm quite ready. Let's get on with it," she had urged.

He had helped her over the edge, found her a toehold, guided her as long as it was possible for him to do so. He was still near her, and it was not as difficult as she had imagined. But, as he had said, the pine needles were a hazard. They carpeted the earth, rubbing against her tee shirt. Worse than that, however, was the roughness of the shrubs against her hands. Her palms were beginning to hurt, and there was more than a small chance that they would be bleeding by the time she reached the bottom. It was not easy to find a toehold. Once or twice she'd needed to depend on her left foot and had felt a nasty twinge in her ankle. The shale was rough against her sneakers. She could feel little pebbles inside them, and it seemed to her that her right toe was exposed, but she dared not think of these minor discomforts. She must concentrate on what she was doing, must grab, pull, hold, grab, pull, hold. It was like doing sit-ups. Stretch, touch toes, lie down. Grab, pull, hold...

"Are you all right, Stacia?" Paul's voice was near, but not as near as it had been at the beginning. He could not remain too close to her. He was now a short distance below her. "Stacia," he repeated edgily. "Are you all right?"

"Fine!" she called. Grab, pull, hold, grab, pull, her hand closed on air. The plant for which she had grabbed was out of reach—but there was a projecting rock. It looked strong enough. What had Paul said about rocks? Some were loosely embedded in the shale, but that particular rock did not seem loose. She caught it— it held firm; she slid down, holding onto it, feeling for a place to put her toe, but she was sliding again, and the rock... *the rock wasn't holding!* It was in her hand; it was too large for her to continue to grasp. The rock was out of her hand, rolling, rolling down the incline, and she was following it, down, down, down, reaching futilely for a small bush, which broke off as she pulled at it, then grabbing a branch that wasn't fastened to anything at all, sliding down, down, down.

"Stacia," Paul yelled. "Oh, my God, Stacia."

There was panic in his tone. It frightened her. She wanted to stop, but she was still sliding, and the pine needles were sticking into her shirt. They were in her hair, too, needles and twigs and... suddenly, she was no longer sliding. She was lying against a huge bush with sharp, prickly leaves. Never mind the fact that they were sharp or prickly or that they had scratched her legs where her jeans were ripped—how they'd been ripped, she couldn't remember now. Anyway, the rips hardly mattered. What mattered was that Paul had told her sliding could be stopped by bushes, and he had been right— a bush had stopped her. She lay there, her face pressed against the shale, gasping with relief and blinking away the tears that threatened to come.

She was vaguely aware that Paul was beside her again, clinging to a bush a few feet away. She managed to look in his direction and saw him reach out a hand to her, but he did not succeed in touching her. "Are . . . you all right?" His voice was not quite steady. "Stacia?"

She had managed to blink back her tears, but was she all right? She was not quite sure. She felt shaken. Her ankle ached dully, but nothing else seemed really hurt. "I'm okay. You—you said I might slide." She found that she could actually smile. "Well, I slid. I—I guess I covered a lot more territory."

"Yes, you did." He sounded relieved, but there was still an edge of anxiety to his tone as he added, "Are you sure you're all right?"

"I'm sure. I—I shouldn't have grabbed for that rock. You warned me about rocks. It was all my own fault."

"Don't be silly!" he said sharply. "You've been doing great—just great. No professional mountaineer could've done any better. But I want you to rest a bit—stay there and rest a few minutes."

"I think I'd rather get to the bottom."

"But . . ." He frowned. "Look, we're in no hurry, you know."

"I understand, but I don't need to rest. I'm fine. Honestly."

"Honestly?" he asked dubiously.

"I assure you—it's the truth, the whole truth and nothing but the truth, so help me, God." No use adding that she was beginning to hate every moment spent on the cliff. No use explaining that anything was better than staying here any longer than was necessary for the descent. Mountain climbers must be born, not made, she thought. She *had* to get down right away—even if it meant another slide.

"All right," he said reluctantly. He added with a grin, "On your mark, get set . . . bang, that's the starting gun."

Stacia moved away from the bush and frowned as she felt something on her face. It wasn't a leaf or a twig; it was too thin and clinging for that. Raising a hand, she brushed at it and knew it was a spider web. "Ugh!" she exclaimed.

"Anything the matter?" Paul called anxiously.

"I just got a spider web on my face," she called. "I only hope the occupant didn't come along for the ride— or slide." She achieved a realistic laugh.

"They don't usually stick around." His tone was comforting.

"Good." She brushed it off and secured another toehold. Grab, pull, hold, grab, pull, hold. Against her will, her fear returned. The pine needles were sticking into her. Her toe was definitely protruding from her right shoe. Her hands were bleeding. Spider webs were good for wounds. Maybe she should have kept her adornment. Where had she heard that about spider webs? She couldn't remember. Her ankle hurt like hell. Grab, pull, hold. How long had she been at this? Would she ever, ever, ever get to the bottom? Grab . . . but she wasn't touching anything. She froze, afraid to look. Dared she try for another rock?

"Stacia." Paul's voice reached her. "Let go."

"Let go?" she croaked, trembling, afraid to look in his direction. "But—"

"I'll catch you."

"B-but you m-mustn't p-put yourself in danger," she said between chattering teeth.

"I'm not in danger, Stacia. I'm on the ground. Look."

She turned her head slowly, almost afraid to believe what he was saying, and saw him standing below her, his arms upraised. Standing! "We have actually . . ."

"We have actually reached the bottom of the cliff," he told her gently. "We've made it, my dear."

"Oh, God," she whispered, and thankfully let go, allowing herself to slide the rest of the way into his arms. She turned toward him blindly. "I—I—I—" Amazingly, her teeth were chattering. Amazingly, she was trembling. "P-P-Paul, I—I—I c-c-can't s-s-stop," she gasped. "I— I—I'm not c-c-cold bu-but I'm shaking. . . . I—I g-g-guess I—I was s-scared. S-sorry to be . . . to be so f-foolish."

"Don't you dare be sorry," he scolded, wrapping his arms around her. "Don't you dare." Lifting her, holding her against him, he sank down and rocked her back and forth in his arms as if she were a frightened child while he murmured soothingly, "It's all right, honey. You were so brave, so very brave, and you're safe now. We've reached the bottom, and you're quite safe." He stroked her hair back from her face.

It was several moments before she could stop trembling—more than several. The spell seemed to last a long time—too long. She should not have given way like that; she never had before. For all his kindness, for all his gentleness, Paul must think her a coward. He must *not* believe her a coward. He could not admire cowards.

And she was not shaking any longer. Her teeth were not chattering, and she could speak, could withdraw from his embrace and look up at him, but she was having difficulty seeing him, because tears were in her eyes. Tears she could not check spilled down her cheeks. "You—you mustn't th-hink that I am a...a coward," she said in a shamed whisper.

"Coward," he repeated huskily. "God, Stacia, that's the last thing I'd think." He slipped his arm around her waist.

"I feel so..." She wiped a hand across her eyes. "I'm not usually so—"

"Stacia, darling," he interrupted. "I want you to see something," Paul said firmly. He pointed "I want you to look up...."

She followed his pointing finger and saw the high cliff directly in front of her. She stared at it dazedly, incredulously. It seemed to stretch up into infinity. "We—we came down *that?*" she whispered.

"None other," he assured her. "That took guts, plain, old-fashioned, unvarnished guts. We..." He turned aside, scanning the surrounding trees. "Oh, my God!" he exclaimed. Suddenly, he too began to shake.

"Paul?" Stacia, still clutched against his quivering body, was alarmed. Had he also succumbed to an attack of whatever had possessed her? No, that was impossible. She had been in some sort of shock—she realized that now—but he, an experienced climber, could not have shared those fears. He—was he laughing? She stared up at him. He was laughing. "Paul, what is it?" she asked.

"Look, darling, look, look, look." Still keeping her in the circle of his arms, he used the other arm to point toward what appeared to be a clump of trees.

Looking in the direction he had indicated, Stacia saw

walls, log walls, a roof made from rough shingles, and, topping it, part of a stone chimney. It was a cabin! "We...we're..." she gasped.

Paul's laughter increased as, moving away from her, he bent and picked up something which had been lying at the base of a nearby tree. Raising it aloft, he said solemnly, "Stacia, I give you civilization!"

Staring at the object in his hand, Stacia too began to laugh. He was holding an old, rusted beer can.

Beer cans notwithstanding, there was a deep silence in these woods and a primeval look to the tall pines and the thick trunks of the mighty oaks. That was borne in upon Stacia even as the echo of Paul's laughter still rang in her ears. Yet certainly, they must be near one of the many trails that bisected the so-called "wilderness" area of the Sierra Nevada range. The cabin was mute witness to that. It also promised shelter. Though she could see from here that the roof was broken, part of it was still intact. It would be a place to stop and rest. She needed rest. There was an "all-gone" feeling inside which she had no trouble diagnosing as one more reaction to that arduous and terrifying descent. She was still a little dazed by it, and by something else.

Paul had been wonderfully tender with her. He had called her "dearest," "honey,"—"darling!" He had spoken as if he meant it. Yet, upon mature reflection, she was ready to accuse herself of attaching far too much importance to both his actions and his words. Naturally, he had been concerned about her—he would have been concerned about anyone undergoing an attack of nerves as violent as hers had been. Remembering it, she gritted her teeth. He must have thought her half demented! He had spoken to her very soothingly—had, in fact, treated her as if she had been a terrified little girl. Such endearments as he had employed were natural, under those circumstances. That was how grown-ups spoke to hysterical kids. What a damned fool she had made of herself! It would not happen again, not if they had to climb down twenty more precipices!

"Stacia."

She jumped. She had forgotten he was standing so close to her. "Yes, Paul?" She smiled at him, hoping that she looked calmer.

"Shall we visit what I hope will be our temporary headquarters?" He pointed to the cabin.

Stacia found that she could laugh. "Please; I'd love to see it. Though it looks as if it might have served as temporary headquarters, too, for the three bears."

"Well," he said solemnly. "Aren't I forearmed? I have Goldilocks with *me*." Giving her hair a playful tweak, he scooped her up in his arms again.

"Paul!" Stacia protested, "I think I can walk."

"And I don't want you putting any more strain on that ankle than is absolutely necessary," he told her sternly. "Just slip your arms around my neck." He lifted one of her hands and then turned it over, staring at the palm. "Good God!" He frowned at her. "Why didn't you tell me about this?"

"About what?"

"What?" he repeated angrily. "Your palm..." He looked at the other hand. "Your palms are bleeding— yes, both of them—and don't tell me you didn't notice."

"Oh." She had a recollection of the stinging pain she had experienced coming down the mountain. "Would you believe that I forgot all about it?"

"No, I wouldn't," he returned harshly. "And please cut the needless heroics. You could get an infection.

We'll need to clean them off." Along with his jacket he had strapped her tote bag to his back, and now he reached for it.

"Not yet," she begged. "Let's look at the cabin first."

"But—"

"Please, Paul. And honestly, I did forget.. That slide I took put everything out of my mind."

His arms tightened briefly. "Okay, I'll buy that." He stared at her a long moment before adding with what seemed an almost spurious lightness, "All right, Madame Goldilocks, I'll show you the property. By the way, we call it Bear Lodge." His smile took a moment to leap from his mouth to his eyes.

Stacia felt herself off center again. For that moment, it had seemed apparent to her that Paul was more shaken by her brush with disaster than she had realized. However, the fact that he had made so obvious an effort to hide that emotion from himself—or was it from her?— was discouraging. But it fit with her earlier conclusions. She must not attach any importance to those moments when he had held her so tightly in his arms, when he had called her "darling" and "dear." Even if those endearments had not been uttered solely in an effort to soothe and comfort her, he was going to remain in control of himself. Gloria was on her mind, and she must certainly be on his. Well, that was as it should be. If Paul had been her fiancée, she would have wanted him to exercise a similar control. After all, they were in an extremely compromising situation. She stifled a sigh. Her thinking was becoming extremely convoluted. She laughed. "You know," she told him, "you're crazy."

He appeared to give her remark careful consideration. "Not crazy, madame. Light-headed is a term I prefer, if you don't mind."

"Not in the least."

"I don't guarantee that this house is in the best condition. The three former tenants, you understand..."

"Just as long as those three tenants have resigned their occupancy," she murmured.

He chuckled. "We shall soon find out." He strode toward the cabin.

She had complained about his carrying her, but she did feel comfortable and so secure in his arms. Stacia frowned. It was unlike her to experience such a feeling. She was not sure she liked it. All of her life, she had hated being dependent upon anyone.

Her father had remarked on that tendency when she was not quite seven. "None of this feminine-mystique bit for our daughter. She was born liberated."

"She takes after me." Her mother had laughed.

Her mother *had* been her own person, but she had also been a very loving wife. It had really been the ideal marriage, and if she were to marry Paul... *marry Paul?* Now who was being light-headed... or *nonheaded?* Why did these ridiculous ideas keep running through what was left of her brain? She had to remember Gloria, for heaven's sake. She had to remember the circumstances under which she and Paul had met. She also had to realize that what she felt for him might not be anything deeper than mere physical attraction!

As a photographer, she had always been attracted to handsome men—for example, George. No, she realized with a pang, in the last few days, Paul's appearance had ceased to matter to her. It was his kindness and consideration for one who, in the beginning, had deserved neither of these. She had never met a man like him. She turned another threatening sigh into a deep breath and thought wryly that she was becoming adept at this type of silent prevarication.

"Ah, madame, *voilà,* we have arrived. Though the

door is closed, it seems to be minus a knob, so I believe
we shall not need our key after all. If I might put madame
down?"

"Mais certainement, monsieur." It took a real effort
for Stacia to smile at Paul. Their time together was drawing to a close. She felt that strongly—as strongly as if
waiting behind that knobless portal was a man, beer can
in hand, ready to announce that his citizen's band radio
would connect them with a trucker whose rig was built
by Curtis—and who would immediately alert Mrs. Curtis
as to their whereabouts.

Paul set her down gently. Indicating a tree stump she
had not noticed, he said, "Sit here." He held out his arm
and, dutifully clutching it, she hopped to the stump.
Watching him move toward the cabin, Stacia ran her
hand through her hair, a habitual gesture whenever she
was disturbed. To her horror, her hair was not only tangled but full of twigs and leaves. She had a brief, unwelcome image of how she must appear. She must look
like a wild-woman.

A downward glance showed that her tee-shirt had
turned from white to muddy brown except where it was
full of green pine needles. Her toe had gone through her
right sneaker, and her left sneaker was also torn on one
side. Her jeans were filthy! She looked longingly at her
tote bag. If only she had remembered to put her compact
in the pocket of her jeans . . . but perhaps it was just as
well she hadn't. She was in no mood for the revelations
of its mirror. In that same instant, she noticed that Paul's
trousers were more then merely torn—they were ragged.
His suede shoes had been totally ruined by the wet and
the climb. His own hair was not free of leaves and twigs,
while a five-day beard bristled on his cheeks and chin.
Unfortunately, it was small comfort to know that they

were equally disreputable-looking. Men expected ... to hell with what men expected! The fact that they had been reduced to a near-primitive mode of life did not warrant her indulging in what was plainly prehistoric thinking. She—

"Not princely, but definitely bearless." Paul's statement cut into her futile reflections. Looking up, Stacia found that he had pushed the cabin door open. Now, to the sound of a rusty squeal from its ancient hinges, he shoved it further back, revealing an interior that showed Stacia that her wild fantasies were groundless, which, of course, she had known already.

Stepping to her side, Paul held out his arms. "Come and survey our castle," he invited with an impish grin.

Hastily putting her weight on her good ankle, Stacia rose. "I'll take your arm."

"With or without the rest of me?" he inquired.

She gave him the sort of long-suffering look such a remark demanded. "I was about to tell you I could hop the rest of the way."

"Very well, but don't put the other one down," he cautioned.

"I am using only my best foot to go forward." She laughed as he groaned and supplied the needed arm. She was glad he had given her no further arguments. For her peace of mind and general well-being, it was imperative that he not carry her over that threshold. Furthermore, she must remember that they had known each other only five days. That wasn't even long enough to grow a decent beard!

"Well," he demanded a moment later, "what do you think of our residence?"

Propped against a rough wall, Stacia grinned as she stared about what was no more than a small room. Once it had boasted a plank floor, but half of that was rotted away, and the dirt beneath had been turned into mud by the recent rain. Generations of spiders had spun and vacated the webs festooning corners high and low. The winds, depositing twigs and branches through the hole in the roof, had also blown in a carpeting of pine needles, some brown and brittle with age, others of recent vintage. Pine cones were scattered among them, and here too, a small animal had met its fate. Judging from its minute skeleton, it had probably been a squirrel. However, on the other side of the cabin, enough roofing remained to provide adequate shelter, and a fireplace was still paved with bricks. If the battered chimney worked, it might be possible to build a fire, come nightfall. With that hole in the roof and the windows on either side of the front door, they would need it.

"It's not much," Paul murmured, "but we call—"

"Don't you dare!" Stacia laughed. Sobering, she added, "I expect it will be okay for the night, unless you'd rather go farther."

"I would not rather," he assured her quickly. "We've done enough traveling for today. You need—"

"A bath," she moaned. "I am filthy. My hair . . . look at it."

"A rich gold," he commented.

"And full of green twigs, pine needles, pebbles, sand and God knows what. I feel like that old man in the Lear poem."

"The one with the beard!" Paul laughed. "I haven't thought of him in years. . . ." Clapping a hand to his chest, he quoted in a sonorous voice, "'It is just as I feared—Two Owls and a . . . a . . .'"

"'Hen,'" Stacia supplied. "'Four Larks and a Wen' . . . no . . ."

"'Wren,'" he supplied, "'Have all built their nests in my beard.'"

"Right." She clapped her hands. "Imagine *your* being acquainted with old Mr. Lear."

"I know him quite well. 'Far and few, far and few, Are the lands...' Can you continue with that?"

"'The lands where the Jumblies live,'" she said glibly. "'Their heads are green, and their hands are blue, And they went to sea in a Sieve.'"

It was his turn to clap, and he did, loudly. "Head of the class again, Stacia."

She flushed, remembering the first time he had said that. Had it been only five days ago?—it seemed like five years, five centuries! She kept her eyes on the floor as she said, "Thank you, kind sir, but I still need a bath."

"Probably there's water nearby. I can't imagine anyone constructing a cabin unless there were some within a reasonable distance. There might have been a stream gleaming with gold, because, unless I miss my guess, this shack was built by a prospector."

"Gold country?" she exclaimed. "Do you think that's where we are?"

"I couldn't swear to it, but I think so. As I told you, ponderosa pines grow farther down, and most of these out here are of that variety. I had an idea we'd landed near the foothills. I'm not familiar with the territory, but I've read that there are lots of places that have been reclaimed by the wilderness."

"I've read that too," she said.

He moved to the sheltered corner of the cabin and, kneeling down, brushed away some of the debris. He took his jacket off and put it on the floor.

"Oh, don't," she protested. "There's still so much dirt..."

He smiled at her. "It has that in common with my jacket. "You sit here, and I'll go out and do some scouting."

"Oh," Stacia groaned. "I wish I could go with you. I feel so absolutely useless!"

"You're not useless, and you're certainly decorative, Lear lady."

He was teasing, of course, but she felt her cheeks grow hot. "Stop it," she scolded. "I know exactly how I must look. Which reminds me. Hand me the tote bag. It's time that I faced the truth."

"The truth?"

"My mirror."

"Mirror, mirror..." He paused, cocking his head.

"What's—" she began.

"Hssst." He put a finger to his lips.

Obediently, Stacia lapsed into silence. She was a little fearful, wondering what he could have heard. There were so many possibilities....She did not even discount bears. Then she heard it too. The unmistakable splash of a waterfall. "Oh!" She held out her hands. "Paul, let's go look for it!" she cried rapturously. She did not protest as he bent down and, lifting her into his arms, strode back across that threshold and out—going in the direction of that lovely sound.

chapter

7

STACIA, STANDING AMIDST thick, high grass, looked appreciatively at the small waterfall gushing over brownish boulders, moss-bearded and gleaming gold in such shafts of sunlight as penetrated the thick canopy of pine and oak branches.

The waters descended into a small pool, which looked to be deep, and then lengthened into a stream. It was a beautiful sight. There was almost too much beauty around her. She and Paul had come through a small meadow heavy with bright orange poppies and tall blue lupines. There were other flowers for which she had no name, and here, between the rocks, bloomed yellow blossoms which Paul had called cinquefoil. Thin blue insects fluttered iridescent wings over the stream, and she could hear the shrill whine of the hordes of mosquitoes which appeared in summer. Fortunately, that was one predator which left her absolutely alone. Explaining it to Paul, Stacia had advanced the theory that, since she had been terribly bitten some years back, the mosquitoes had run up a flag saying, "territory claimed."

"I seem to be immune to them too," he had told her. "Raoul Mackintosh, a French-Canadian friend of mine, said it was my bad blood. But either way, we're damned lucky—because without any spray to ward them off, we could be eaten alive."

Lucky, most certainly. They were lucky to be alive, lucky to have survived five days in this wilderness, when she was incapacitated by her ankle—and she was lucky to have Paul caring for her. Not so lucky to be in love with him.

"Don't think about that, Stacia," she muttered, looking downstream and not seeing him because of the intervening bushes and the meandering path of the waters. He had left her to the waterfall, while he went looking for trout. She was grateful to him for that—sensing that he was anxious about her and would have preferred to remain with her while she bathed. She had definitely not wanted him there.

This was due less to modesty than to the fact that she had what even George had not hesitated to describe as a perfect figure. Everything was in proportion—from her breasts, not large, but beautifully formed, to her small waist and slender hips. Much as she was attracted to Paul, she did not want to play the role of Eve, the temptress. And for two good reasons: either he would be able to resist her or he wouldn't! If he could withstand the temptation she presented, it would be a disaster for her ego. If he could not, it might be disastrous for him, leaving him full of assorted guilts. No, if she were to be entirely honest, there was another reason why she did not want to set a sensuous trap for him. It would only result in her own confusion, and possibly deep hurt, too. She wanted him to make love to her, but she wanted the lovemaking to be based on more than mere physical attraction.

Stacia had a moment of wishing she were Anne Harte. Anne would never have indulged in such soul-searchings. She would have made sure that Paul was watching before she struck so much as a finger in the water. Anne . . . never mind Anne; she needed to take that bath now—or he would be back before she was ready. She had already slipped out of her torn and dirt-encrusted jeans. She took off her tee shirt and unfastened her bra, shivering a little as the cool breezes seemed to encircle her naked body. She reached for her terry-cloth robe but did not put it around her. She slid toward the pool, cursing her sore ankle. If she could have stood up, she could have gotten wet by degrees instead of needing to immerse her whole body at once. She had already toe-tested the water, and received the impression that its source must be the South Pole. Joking aside, she was sure that it was a glacier-fed stream originating high in the mountains—but one would have expected it to have become warmer in its travels from those ice-bound peaks. She had never experienced anything so cold. Paul had warned her not to remain in the water too long, but she didn't need a warning; she could not stay in there long. In fact . . . She sighed. In the interests of cleanliness, in the interests of five day's worth of inadequate sponge baths, she must take the plunge.

"Do it quickly, Stacia," she muttered to herself. "Quickly!"

She rolled off the bank and into the water. With difficulty, she suppressed the scream which might have brought Paul running. The water was even colder than her toe-test had indicated. The rocks at the edge of the pool were slippery and hard against her flesh. She moved away, and unexpectedly went down below the surface into really deep water. Water? She was swimming in recently melted ice! The cold seemed to penetrate to her very bones, frosting them under her skin. As Stacia popped to the surface, her teeth were chattering, and she knew she must be turning blue. A couple of minutes later, she decided that numbness must have set in. She felt much better and, if not warm, at least reasonably comfortable. The chill waters were proving to be wonderfully refreshing. Making her way toward the waterfall, she let its drops comb through her matted hair. Thrusting her fingers into the tangled strands, she extricated twigs and leaves and worked out some of the knots. As she treaded water, she wished that the pool were wider, so that she could really swim. However, it was beginning to feel cold again, and Paul had warned that the moment she felt shivery, she must get out.

She was about to follow his advice, when she heard a crashing sound through the thickets to her left. She blushed. Had Paul returned already? Glancing in the direction of the sound, it occurred to her that he would not have come from that side. More crashing noises reached her ears. The bushes were moving. Someone was coming toward the bank of the stream. Keeping her eye on that spot, she sank down into deep water, mentally upbraiding herself for not having considered the possibility that hikers were in the area. At this time of the year, hikers, backpackers and even boy scouts hit the mountain trails, and if, as Paul contended, they had really come into gold country, the woods could be filled with campers.

It was beginning to be very cold in her watery hiding place. Stacia, positioned close to the waterfall, watched nervously as the bushes were parted by whatever was coming through it. She had discarded her theories about boy scouts or hikers. Undoubtedly, the intruder was some manner of thirsty animal—probably a deer—but just as she reached this conclusion, she saw a huge furry brown shape, and a moment later, she was staring into the small eyes of an immense bear.

Stacia screamed, and screamed again. The bear, opening its mouth to expose a lolling red tongue set between two gleaming white fangs, growled deep in its throat. To Stacia's terrified eyes, the animal looked as if it could ford the stream in two steps. An instant vision of the Central Park Zoo reminded her that bears did not mind paddling about in the water. Another scream...

"Stacia..." Paul's voice was faint. Obviously, he was some distance downstream. "What is it?"

"B-b-bear!" she cried as loudly as she could. At the same time, the bear shook its huge head and, turning, lumbered back through the foliage. It was cold, incredibly cold, in the water, but Stacia could not bring herself to emerge. If the beast were to return... She had a vivid memory of what had happened to some campers in Sequoia National Park one year.

"Bear?" Paul yelled. He was closer now. He came through the shrubbery on the right bank.

"Watch out," she cried through chattering teeth.

"Where is it?"

She raised a trembling hand and pointed at the foliage on the opposite bank. "It—it was there."

"Not any more," he said. "You probably scared it off."

"S-scared it off?"

"Bears are generally shy of people, and for good reason." He looked hard at her and added quickly, "You'd best come out. You must be freezing."

"I...I..." She shook her head. Quite suddenly, she felt as if the water had congealed. She could not move, and then, to her horror, she felt herself sinking. She wanted to explain, but the words stuck in her throat.

"Stacia!" Paul waded into the water and, seizing her by the arm, pulled her up, carrying her back to the bank. "Good God!" He stared at her. "You are practically purple with cold." Hastily, he wrapped her in her robe, rubbing her vigorously. "You need to be in front of a fire," he said urgently. "Else you might catch your death of cold. Wait; I'll be right back."

"Don't l-leave me," she wailed.

"I'll only be a minute or so," he promised. "I've got to get our dinner before Bruno sniffs it out—and also, there are my clothes."

"Oh." For the first time, she became aware of the fact that Paul was also naked. She looked down quickly. "Of course," she said.

"Don't be afraid," he said. "I'm sure that bear won't be back to trouble you." He hurried away.

Shivering, Stacia got back into her jeans and tee shirt. Even dressed, she was still conscious of an intense coldness, one that had nothing to do with bodily temperature, or maybe it did. His. She could almost laugh at her former fears. Perfect figure or not, he had not even noticed it—but, her rational self assured her, she had not noticed that he was undressed either. Still...

"Come." Paul's return ended her speculations. He was carrying another trout. He thrust it at her with a smile. "You take this and I'll take you."

He carried her back to the cabin, walking through the beautiful meadow under the warming sun. One arm around his neck, the other outstretched, holding the trout, Stacia imagined the picture they must present. Adam bearing Eve back to their rude shelter, but an Adam who was in love with another Eve, named Gloria.

Something awakened Stacia. Opening her eyes, she was momentarily confused. She had half expected to see the rocky ceiling of the cave. Memory returned in an instant. She had a vision of Paul building the fire that still crackled on the grate.

They had eaten the trout and some mushrooms that Paul had sworn were not toadstools. He had been very silent during the meal. She guessed that he was probably as tired as she felt. She was sure of it when he suggested that they try to sleep, even though it was just a little past five and the sun was shining through the windows.

"You've had a hard day," he had told her. "And it might be even harder tomorrow. We'll have to be on our way."

He had spoken about looking for trails, but she had only the vaguest memory of what had been said. She barely remembered getting undressed. Undressed? Hadn't she slept in her clothes?

No; Paul had told her they were too damp. (Had he eased them off and pulled her tee shirt over her head?) She flushed. She had a vague recollection of his bringing her her nightgown.

"Put this on," he had commanded curtly. Curtly? Had he been curt? Yes.

After she obeyed, he had put her robe about her.

"It's dry," she recalled telling him.

"I hung it by the fire," he explained.

She had been confused by that, wondering what he had hung it on, but she had been too weary to wonder much. She had another vague memory, of his shaking out his jacket and spreading leaves on the floor and telling her to lie down. She must have fallen asleep that first second. No, it had been the *second* second. She recalled his stretching out beside her, pulling her against him, recalled having been grateful for his closeness and knew immediately why she had awakened. The warm, comforting length of his body was no longer beside her. She was alone!

Stacia sat up, looking around her. Darkness was framed in the small windows on either side of the door.

A wind blew cold through the hole in the roof. Stacia was concerned. Where had Paul gone? Why had he left her? She felt bereft. Oddly, it seemed to her as if some portion of herself had gone with him. She did not feel complete without him. She grimaced. That was the way Nadine Brewer, an *Eyeview* editor, had described her divorce.

"I ought to feel bitter toward Charlie, but all I am is lonely. It's as though I'd been cut in half."

Stacia had been more contemptuous than sympathetic. No one ought to be that dependent upon another person, especially a man. She had wanted to say, "You leaned on him too much. That doesn't spell happiness in this day and age." Of course, she had held her tongue, which had been just as well, because before the decree had become final, Nadine was back with Charlie. When Stacia had last seen them, they seemed to be happy—thus shooting her theory all to hell.

That had nothing to do with her situation. She was leaning on a man who had absolutely no interest in her, as witness his response—or, rather, his lack of response—by the waterfall. There was something else she must remember—she had done nothing to invite a response. If she had . . . would he have . . . ?

"Damn," she muttered, "stop it. You're acting like a teenager in the throes of first love."

No, she was not being fair to herself or to her feelings. As she had already decided, they were not based on mere physical attraction. She and Paul had a great deal more in common than that. She liked the way his mind worked. She smiled, thinking about their mutual interest in the works of Edward Lear. Stacia was positive that the more they spoke, the more plots of common ground they would find. Unfortunately, they would not have that opportunity. Tomorrow or the next day, they would discover a trail which would lead them to civilization.

Anne Harte had once complained that all the best men seemed to have been grabbed up when they were scarcely out of their cradles. Paul had been around considerably longer. If only they had met under happier circumstances. "If wishes were horses..." Stacia sighed and looked at the door. Where had he gone, and why? Had something aroused him? Had he wanted to investigate? How long had he been gone?

Clutching at the wall of the cabin, Stacia pulled herself up and moved against it until she reached the door. She pushed it back and gazed out upon beauty. The moon was up—high and milk-white in a star-encrusted sky. Its rays streaked the tops of the tall firs and cast the shadows of their wind-tossed branches upon the ground. A chorus of crickets and frogs was loud in her ears, and there were other sounds—the peeps, squeaks, shrieks and burbles of nameless night creatures living and, perhaps, dying in the darkness. Stacia did not see Paul. Where could he be?

The image of the bear arose in her mind. Had it come prowling around the cabin? Had Paul gone to drive it away, and had it proved dangerous, turning upon him? Was he lying out there in the windy night, bleeding or... Panic drove his name to her lips. "Paul," she called loudly. "Paul, where are you?"

There was the crackling of leaves on the ground. Paul came through the trees and stepped into a shimmering pool of moonlight. He looked strange, almost ghost-like, his brown eyes cavernous in his whitened face. "Stacia," he said, "why are you on your feet?" He spoke peremptorily. He sounded angry. That did not matter. He was there and he was unharmed.

"I missed you. I thought you might have heard the bear."

He laughed mirthlessly. "No, but there are other dangers around."

"Others? Why seek them out? Please come back."

"Maybe I left because..." He paused. Anger threaded his tones again. "You must go inside, Stacia. The moonlight..." He stopped.

"The moonlight?" she questioned. "I don't understand." That was not quite true. She had a feeling that she did understand.

"Damn you, you should," came his corroborating exclamation. "You should know how it is to be near you, Stacia... you should know how you look in the moonlight, with your hair turned silver and your skin silver and your eyes..." He broke off. "For God's sake, go inside."

There was a throbbing deep in her throat. There was a growing happiness inside of her; it was keeping pace with her yearning to have him with her. "Paul," she whispered. "Please, come back with me."

"You don't know..."

"I do." She dared to part from the sustaining doorway. She put her sore foot on the ground and, oblivious to the twinges of pain traveling up her leg, came toward him. "Paul, I need you with me. I need *you*." She stretched out her hands.

A sound that seemed to begin as a protest but which ended in a soft, triumphant laugh broke from him. "Do you, Stacia?"

He seized her hands, pulled her against him. Holding her so tightly that she could feel the pounding of his heart through the thin material of her nightgown, he kissed her. It was a long, slow, searching kiss. When he lifted his head, Stacia, winding her arms around his neck, opened her mouth for a second kiss. It lasted even longer than the first, and at its end, he lifted her in his arms and, holding her against him, bore her into the cabin.

The fire was nearly out, but its fitfull glow was enough to light his way to their makeshift couch. Gently, but urgently, Paul released her clinging arms and put her down. In that dim glow, Stacia watched him swiftly take off his clothing. His naked body, turned coppery by the dying fire, looked like a bronze statue, but bronze was cold to the touch, and when he knelt beside her, his flesh was warm, warm against her, as he eased her nightgown off.

"If you only knew how very much I have wanted you, darling," he said huskily, his eyes roving over her body. "Today by the stream, I had to fight against taking you."

"I wanted you too," she whispered. "I thought . . . I thought you didn't want me."

"Oh, God," he groaned. "I have been in hell, needing you."

"It's a hell I've shared." She caressed his cheek and ran a finger over the line of his eyebrows.

Seizing her hand, he pressed a fervent kiss into her palm. "Stacia," he whispered.

She was glad that the fire was not completely out— because without its light, she would have been unable to see his eyes. Never, she realized, would she have believed that Paul could look at her so ardently and yet so tenderly.

"Stacia, Stacia, Stacia . . . I love to say your name." He stretched out beside her. "It's beautiful, and you are beautiful, incredibly beautiful—something out of a dream. I can scarcely believe we're together at last."

"You can believe it," she murmured with an excited

little laugh. "I'll make you believe it, dearest. And..." She grew silent as she felt his exploring lips on her ear, her cheek, her mouth. She pressed herself against him, running her hands up and down the satin smoothness of his back. In another moment, his kisses were falling on the pulsing base of her throat, then moving down to linger on her breasts.

Stacia felt her nipples hardening as his tongue delicately circled first one and then the other. His caresses, ranging over her whole body, awakened responses she had never experienced before. Lying beneath him, she realized she had never been so excited... more than excited—utterly transported! His combination of gentleness and passion was a revelation to her. Eagerly, she returned kiss for kiss, caress for caress, instinctively realizing and fulfilling his every need. Her own excitement was mounting, mounting. Rapturously, she awaited his possession, responding to him joyfully, holding nothing back.

Finally, the beautiful rhythm began. "Paul...Paul..." she murmured, and moving in time to it, she strained against him, reveling in the desire that was quickening his breathing.

"I need you, need you, need you..." she whispered, wild for the feel of him deep inside of her.

His breath was coming in great ragged gasps. She moaned and cried out as she reveled in the thrusting hardness, the driving invasion and the incredible excitement of joining, merging and climaxing into an undreamed-of dimension of ecstacy.

Later, there was the excitement of lying close, close, close against him and falling asleep in his arms—only to awaken to his murmured endearments and the knowledge of a need that she, too, shared and was eager to fulfill again—and yet again.

Stacia awakened to an assault of light and sound. The one coming through the hole in the roof struck her directly in the eyes, and the other was harsh in her ears, harsh, grating and yet not without a certain rhythm. As the last vestiges of sleep departed, she made out words:

> Oh, Susanna, oh,
> Don't you cry for me,
> For I'm gwine to Alabama with my
> Banjo on my knee.

Confused, Stacia raised herself on her elbow and looked around the cabin, wondering if she had dreamed the singing, for it had ceased abruptly, but a second later it was replaced by a "Hello, feller. My, you gave me a start. Where'd you come from?"

"Back there."

Though the answer was brief and couched in tones far less carrying than those of the questioner, Stacia, recognizing the cadences of the voice, was bathed from head to toe in a warmth that had nothing to do with the bright beams filtering through the hole in the roof. Coupled with that was a vibrant sense of well-being which was unlike anything she had ever experienced before. It seemed to her that for the first time in her life, she had learned the real definition of "rapture." It had been beautiful being with Paul—exquisitely, almost unbearably beautiful, because it had been a sharing, rather than a taking, as it had been with George. Not only had Paul been a wonderful, skilled lover; he had been marvelously considerate, seeing her as a partner in delight rather than a receptacle for his pleasure.

"How far?" Paul asked. He must be nearer now, for she could hear him more clearly.

"Not far, mister..." came the answer. There was wonder in the harsh tones as the man continued, "An' you say you come down that-there cliff?"

"That's right," Paul replied.

"An' whereabouts did you land?...I mean when the plane come down."

"I'm not sure. I'd say it was about three or four miles from here." Paul spoke a little uncertainly.

"Well, you sure as hell were lucky, comin' down so close to the foothills. Might've been up near the snow line. It's no joke this time of year; cold as a polar bear's rear end, even in midsummer."

"I know." Paul laughed. "But where are we?"

"Well, you're rightly in what's left of a town useta be called Hellbent."

"Hellbent?" Paul questioned dubiously. "I never heard of that."

"It's a ghost town, mister. Might call it the ghost of a ghost town. T'aint much more left'n that-there cabin and assorted sticks'n stones. Don't ask me where it got its moniker. Probably from some poor soul that was hell-bent on pannin' gold from the stream. Guess there was a couple cabins and maybe a tradin' post, but it's way off the beaten track, even for the bikers."

"The bikers. I've heard you're getting a lot of those up in the foothills." Stacia heard disdain in Paul's voice.

"More all the time. Damned noise of their motors gets to you. So do they. Lot of 'em play rough."

"I know about them." Paul emitted a mirthless laugh. "Hell-bent for Hellbent."

"They don't usually get up this far, though. Nothin' much here to attract 'em, praise the Lord. Let's hope you don't run afoul of 'em, mister, but you look like you can lick your weight in wildcats. You gotta be tough, to do what you done."

The voices were much closer. Stacia glanced around the cabin and saw her clothes hanging on a nail by the fireplace. Hastily, she rose and grabbed them. They were still slightly damp, but not enough to matter. Hastily, she pulled them on. She had a brief moment of regret, wishing that whoever was outside had not arrived. He sounded informed, and that was helpful. However, it would have been more helpful if she could have faced Paul alone this first morning, this important morning, which might be a beginning of . . . what? She hadn't gotten all that sorted out yet. Of course, she could stay inside until whoever it was had left, but she could not, because of her active, reporter's sense of curiosity.

That old feeling of a misplaced heart beating in her throat was present as Stacia drew back the door and came out into the bright white light, to see Paul standing with a grizzled old man, who was clad in what appeared to be army discards from World War II.

He wore a much-patched and -mended khaki shirt. Shabby, olive-drab trousers were thrust into thick, scuffed boots, and a short, Eisenhower jacket hung over his shoulders. He wore a shapeless felt hat pushed down on shaggy, shoulder-length white hair, and around one wrist, she caught the gleam of blue and silver. A second glance showed Stacia that it was a heavy turquoise-and-silver Indian bracelet. His face was burned dark brown, and the myriad lines around his eyes and etched into his forehead and by the sides of his mouth made her wonder if he might not be a veteran of the *First* World War. His eyes, small and bright under tufted brows, widened as she emerged. "Waal, good mornin', miss." He grinned appreciatively.

Paul turned quickly, and it seemed to Stacia that his whole body stiffened. However, he said casually enough, "Hi, honey."

"Good morning." Stacia divided her smile between the two men. She had thought her heart would go back to its proper place, but it was still in her throat and pounding harder than ever as she looked at Paul. She felt her cheeks grow warm and feared she must be blushing like a schoolgirl. It was ridiculous to feel shyness creeping over her. Once, she had been very shy, but between that time and this stretched five years of being a reporter—five years' of interviews with the famous and not-so-famous. These had helped her to conquer that feeling, but it was certainly back with her this morning! Shyness... and a rather mad sort of excitement, too.

All at once, she was glad of the stranger's presence. It was making this first ordinary encounter in broad daylight after abandoned intimacy in the deep night easier... or more casual... or something. She was still all too aware of that tightening of Paul's body at her arrival. Was he having second thoughts about last night? Was he regretting their passionate murmurings to each other. Their ecstatic lovemaking? A cold apprehension was taking the place of the happiness which had flooded through her upon awakening. She remembered Paul in the moonlight, remembered his reluctance and *her* insistence that he come back into the cabin. She had imagined she was responding to his response to her as much as to her own. But perhaps it had been merely a "reflex" on his part, the normal male reaction to an attractive woman making herself available. Or was it just plain silly to have this deluge of doubts merely because she'd noticed—or thought she'd noticed—a drawing back in him that had not been present in the night?

"Honey," Paul said. "This is Jeb Craik. He's a prospector. Mr. Craik, my wife."

Shock went through Stacia. She threw a startled glance at Paul and read warnings in his eyes. She guessed that the introduction had been offered in deference to Mr. Craik's white hairs. "Hello." She smiled.

"Hello, there." The old man's quick grin revealed that he had a vein of gold in his teeth, if nowhere else. "I been talkin' to your husband, here. You had quite an experience up in them mountains, seems."

"Yes." She nodded, realizing that all the bad, the frightening, experiences had been blotted from her mind by what had taken place last night.

"You got hurt."

"A bit." She glanced down at her ankle. She had even forgotten about that. Now she realized, though, that it did not hurt as much as it had yesterday.

"How is your ankle this morning, darling?" Paul asked.

"Very much better, thanks." She smiled warmly at him, then shifted her gaze to the old man. "You're a prospector, Mr. Craik? I didn't realize that there was much gold left in these hills."

"Oh, there's some. It's in the streams, too. 'Round here, specially."

"And 'here' is called Hellbent?"

"Right." He grinned again.

"I've always heard there were a lot of forgotten ghost-towns in the foothills of the Sierra Nevadas," she said.

"That's right, ma'am," Craik agreed. "As I was tellin' your husband, hardly nobody comes up this far."

"But," Paul said, smiling at her, "there's a ranger's station about fifteen miles down the trail."

"Is there? Well, that's good news," Stacia said brightly.

"Guess you folks'll be glad to get back to civilization, all right. You sure-enough had some experience."

Stacia glanced at Paul but did not catch his eye. "Yes," she agreed. "It *was* 'some experience.'"

"I ain't much on flyin' myself. I like my feet on the ground." Craik rolled his eyes. "Far's I'm concerned, the sky's for the birds." He emitted a dry chuckle. "In more ways'n one."

"I guess you can say that." A faint smile touched Paul's lips. "But sometimes, it's not so easy to keep your feet on the ground even while you're standing on it."

"That's true enough," Craik said.

It was silly to wonder exactly what Paul meant and to hope he meant what she wanted to believe. And why did she seek definitions for his every casual remark? Because nothing seemed casual any more. Stacia had not wanted the night to end, she remembered, but all nights ended, and sunlight was never as kind as moonlight. It was too strong, too revealing. Paul was full of regrets. She was sure of that. And Gloria, whose name she wished she could blot out of her consciousness, was haunting her as, she was unhappily positive, his fiancée must be haunting Paul.

The ranger's station was only fifteen miles down the road. They were only fifteen miles from civilization. In a very short time, they would be able to send a message to Paul's mother and to Gloria Mannon Meade, his bride-to-be. Was she still Paul's "bride-to-be," or did he have other intentions? No. Even though he had called her his "wife," Stacia was positive that he had no ideas along that line. In fact, he was withdrawing from her. She felt it. She saw it in the way he didn't look at her, and in spite of the warmth of his smile, there was no corresponding gleam in his eyes. Undoubtedly, he was regretting what had taken place. Futhermore, she must remember that it had been at her instigation!

She had to say something. She asked, "Are you going to put us on the right track, Mr. Craik?"

"Yep, me'n Maisie'll point out the route to you," he responded.

"Maisie?"

"My burro. She's around about, croppin' grass. Guess you'll be glad to hear that the trail's nearly downhill all the way."

"Downhill all the way," Stacia repeated, and forced a smile. Inside, that expression caused her a pained grimace. Jeb Craik was talking about the road, she thought unhappily. She glanced at Paul but failed to catch his eye, as he was looking in another direction. Probably he would always be looking in another direction until they reached the ranger's station.

chapter

8

"HERE'S TO CIVILIZATION!" Paul raised one of the tin cups which had come from the large leather knapsack Jeb Craik had strapped to the back of Maisie, his little gray burro, now contentedly cropping grass a few feet away from them.

"Civilization," Stacia echoed with an assumption of the enthusiasm Paul seemed to demand.

"You won't get me drinkin' to that," Jeb growled. "Down the hatch," he added.

The liquid in the cup was, amazingly, coffee, and with it, there was bread, baked fresh that morning in Jeb's stove. His cabin, he had said vaguely, lay down there. He had gestured at a sweep of trees at the bottom of the hill. "I'd let you folks use it," he had explained, "if I could tell you rightly where 'twas, but it's too damned difficult. You might get yerself lost just lookin' for it. Anyhow, when you come down the trail a piece, you'll be runnin' into another of these-here lost towns 'n' you'll find a couple more shacks. They'll be a sight better'n the one you was stuck in last night."

Stacia felt a pain in her heart. Already, "last night" seemed robbed of reality. It was tomorrow morning with a vengeance. Paul was being pleasant, charming and distant, a world away from her. Of course, he had little choice. He could hardly pour "sweet nothings" into her ears, hardly throw her to the ground and make passionate love to her under the nose of the elderly prospector. Still, he could have sent signals; there were such things as warm embracing glances and intimate smiles and . . . but why list the ways, when Paul was so obviously unwilling to avail himself of the means? His sights were evidently set on the civilization he had so enthusiastically toasted with the coffee.

Of course, there was another excuse for him, and that was the breakfast Jeb Craik had provided. She had to remember that most men had what amounted to a holy reverence for this first meal of the day—and poor Paul had been forced into breaking his last fasts with strange grasses. It had been good bread and good coffee, tasting even better, she knew, because of the makeshift nature of their diet for the last five days. Today was their sixth in the wilderness, she remembered. By their eighth, they might have reached the ranger's station—if her ankle were equal to that much walking. It felt much better, but probably she would be wiser to insist on taking at least four more days to reach the station. That would also mean three more nights.

With some difficulty, she suppressed the quiver of excitement that threatened to run the length of her body. It was ridiculous, she decided angrily, to be experiencing such sensations when the reason for them was sitting across from her, his entire attention fixed on a piece of bread, or to put it another way, completely and deliberately ignoring her. Breakfast rituals notwithstanding, Paul was definitely being aloof. Doubtless he had reached the conclusion that she was entirely responsible for his seduction. And, she thought grimly, it was probably true. She had not hesitated to let her needs be known.

* * *

"There she lies," Jeb Craik said. He was pointing to the narrow trail up which he had come. "It runs near a stream; you'll come upon it when you go 'round that bend. You just follow it'n presently you'll be over the borders of Hellbent an' into Absinthe Hollow."

"Absinthe Hollow," Paul repeated with a chuckle. "I've heard of Poker Flat, Brandy Hill and Whiskey Diggings, but I've never heard of Absinthe Hollow. That's sort of a refined drink for up here, isn't it?"

"'Tweren't much of a camp. To the best of my knowledge, it didn't have a long life. They had themselves a placer-minin' operation, but it didn't hardly pay 'em to set up the machinery. Folks swarmed in'n swarmed out like bees without a queen. That's the story of a lot of these-here towns—ghosts almost afore they was built. Anyhow, you keep on goin' down an' you'll find you a shack to stay in—an' eventually, you'll get to the ranger's station'n send your messages. After that, 'tisn't much farther to one of them bigger towns, where you can get yourself some transportation."

"And then home." Paul smiled at Stacia.

She had an answering smile for him. But her heart plummeted as she defined the meaning behind his pleased expression. Probably he was thinking of Gloria Mannon Meade. Maybe, Stacia thought, last night she had been only a stand-in for his fiancée. No, she did not believe that. He had said . . . but she did not want to think about what he had said last night.

"I guess you folks'll get a royal welcome." Craik grinned. "Probably everybody thinks you've croaked up there, 'specially after what happened to that search plane you told me about. Poor man. Like I told you, I never could abide flyin', myself. If we was meant to do it—we'd've been born with wings."

"There's that theory," Paul agreed. He turned to Stacia, slipping an arm around her waist. "I guess since we don't have wings, we'd better be hitting that trail." He added anxiously, "How's your ankle, honey? Do you think you can walk?"

"I'm sure I can for a while," she replied. Had the day suddenly grown brighter, she wondered, or was it the pleasure of that encircling arm and the very real warmth of the smile turned on her?

"You're sure?" He still looked anxious. "Because we'll need to go single file."

"I'll let you know if I have any pain," she assured him.

"And at the first twinge," he said. *"Promise!"*

"Cross my heart and hope to die." She smiled.

"You'd better stick to the shade trees as much as possible," Craik advised. "It'll be heatin' up plenty, come later on this mornin'. You sure as hell won't need them jackets."

Paul's gaze shifted to Craik. "I know. I'm going to make a bundle of them. Give my your jacket, Stacia."

As she shrugged out of it, she felt a surge of annoyance. Mr. Craik had a marvelous sense of timing. His shattering of their brief moment of intimacy had been right on target. A split second later, she knew she was being totally unreasonable in resenting the presence of the old man. Unrealistic, too. They had to get back, and he had pointed the way. It was just that she wished he had made his appearance a little later in the morning, so that she could have a few uninterrupted moments alone with Paul. However, things like that could not be ordered, and the man was well-meaning. That was not always the way with strangers met by chance in the wilderness. With that in mind, she found she could be just as enthusiastic as Paul some twenty minutes later, when they finally parted from him.

"He's a real character," Paul said as they went down the trail. "He'd be good in a novel."

"He's been in a novel." Stacia laughed. "Not to mention the short stories of Bret Harte and Mark Twain."

"That's right. This is their country. It must have been something else in those days."

She nodded. "Gold fever."

"That was a real sickness. It still is."

She caught the edge of bitterness to his tone that she had heard before. There was something troubling him. She wondered what it was—wondered if she would ever know. A time limit had been set—in three or four days...

"Stacia." Paul turned back to her. "Remember that you promised to let me know if you felt the slightest pain in that ankle."

"You've strapped it beautifully. It feels fine."

"Now..." Moving closer to her, he dropped a kiss on her cheek. "Don't be brave, please."

"I've already given you my promise," she reminded him. "Don't you trust me?"

He had been smiling, but at her question, his eyes turned grave. "You've managed to confuse me, my darling."

"How?" she asked breathlessly.

"I couldn't begin to enumerate all the ways. Or rather, I could, but I think that the inevitable discussion will have to postponed until the next rest period. Do you mind?"

"Yes, but I agree."

"Good girl." Abruptly, he wheeled around, saying over his shoulder, almost curtly, "Let's go. And for God's sake watch your step."

She would have liked to call out that his confusion was catching, but the chairman had brought his gavel down and the subject was definitely closed—at least for the time being. But what had he meant, and how should she assess his attitude? Probably she should let it alone for now. Once more she wished she had awakened to his presence beside her in the cabin. No use thinking about that; she hadn't. Consequently, complications had set in—or had they?

She had wanted signals. Well, she had received some. He was concerned about her, concerned and confused, but he had kissed her—only on the cheek, it was true, and lightly, but not as lightly as he could have. If she had been able to weigh that kiss, she would have classified it as a little heavier than a really light kiss; a little heavier, a little warmer, a little more lingering . . . and, of course, she was being adolescent and ridiculous. Something pulled at her sleeve. Startled, she looked up and found she had walked into the overhanging branch of a live oak tree. Flushing, she freed her shirt. She had to look where she was going, and besides, the sights meeting her eyes were worth seeing.

The territory around them was lovely. They had reached the stream, and its silvery waters flowed and bubbled over rocks that seemed to have veins of gold in them. The banks were bordered with ferns and bright wildflowers. Gazing at it, Stacia longed for her lost camera.

If she had her Nikon, she could have captured the tall fir trees, their sweeping branches hung with cones as numerous as Christmas tree ornaments. There were huge cedars, dark against the incredible azure of the sky, and everywhere she looked were flowers—clumps of lilies, azaleas and bushes starred with tiny white blossoms for which she had no name. All of a sudden, a small gray lizard, its scales turned iridescent by the sun, darted out. It skittered away as speedily, but she could have caught it with her lens, caught the birds that winged overhead, the screeching bluejays and the red-winged blackbirds. A squirrel running down the reddish bark of a nearby pine tree would have made a lovely shot—but inevitably, unavoidably, her eyes came back to the man who strode in front of her and the loss of her Nikon was shoved into the back of her mind.

Paul was walking with his head down as if he were thinking, or perhaps he was only taking his own advice and watching where he was going. According to what he had told her earlier, he was probably doing both. She wondered if she filled his thoughts the way he was dominating hers. She regretted the loss of peace of mind she had cultivated so carefully after her ego had recovered from the blows dealt it by George. In the last months, she had tried for a middle level of emotion—but in the short space of a morning, she had dropped to the depths and risen to the heights. She was no longer used to this mental chaos. She had forgotten, or rather, she had tried to put out of her mind, the uncertainties that love could engender. Love? Stacia made a face. She might be putting too large an interpretation on what had happened last night—no, not as far as she was concerned. She did love Paul—but he... She glanced down at her ankle. It was bearing up remarkably well, but she would always tell him that it hurt. Had they been walking long enough for it to hurt? Long enough for her to demand a rest period? She started to call to him but changed her mind. In a sense, that would be cheating, and they weren't walking for their health; they had to cover ground. Around several corners, civilization, in the shape of a forest ranger, awaited them.

She winced, thinking how she had behaved toward
Paul in the beginning. It was a fact she could not avoid,
and there was no use mourning for the time she had
wasted in giving him every reason to despise her. She
had been shrewish, unreasonable and utterly impossible.
Surely, he would remember that. Surely...

"Stacia," Paul said.

"Yes." She stopped and saw that he, too, had stopped,
his head cocked. "What is it?"

"Do you hear that?"

Images of growling bears, roaring mountain lions and
hissing rattlesnakes filled her interior vision as she joined
him. However, her attention was deflected as she saw
that they were approaching a large clearing. "I wonder
if we've come to Absinthe Hollow," she said.

"Shhh," he returned.

"What do you think you hear?" she asked.

"Listen."

She was quiet, straining her ears, and then she heard
it, a roaring sound—a motor? Yes, unmistakably a motor, and it was coming closer—or they were. It seemed
too loud to be just one car, or maybe it was a truck or
a jeep, but it couldn't have been any of these. In spite
of the fact that they were in a clearing, the trees still
grew dense around the trail, and no really large vehicle
could have come up here. "Yet I don't think it's a plane,"
she mused out loud.

"No." Paul shook his head. He added, "I didn't think
we'd be meeting them this far up."

"What?"

"Bikers."

"Oh, I heard you and Jeb talking about them this
morning. Could they really come all the way up here?"

"I don't know. I don't know what 'here' looks like

farther down, but I got the impression from Craik that it was a pretty steep grade."

"That would be dangerous, wouldn't it?"

"Yes, it would, but of course, a lot of bikers thrive on danger, and they're all crazy about challenges. I know. I went through a motorcycle period myself."

The sound was definitely nearer than it had been a couple of minutes ago. Stacia was conscious of a deep regret. They were no longer going to meet civilization. It would soon be joining them. She would imagine what Paul must be thinking, and she might as well agree with him. She said, "I guess maybe we can thumb a ride back to the ranger's station."

His eyes widened. "I hadn't thought of that," he said slowly. He moved a few steps away from her. "But it's a great idea. It'd certainly cut our traveling time down, and more important, it would take the weight off your ankle."

Stacia swallowed. Swallowing didn't do any good. It did absolutely nothing to displace the huge lump in her throat. She had guessed wrong. Out of her own damned insecurities, she had been afraid that he was in a rush to get back, and she had been wrong, wrong, wrong. Getting a ride with the bikers hadn't even crossed his mind. He had been quite content to go the way they were going—the leisurely, beautiful way that would have brought them the better part of a week together in the wilderness. Now there was a different scenario in the works. They would whizz down the incline, and probably by this afternoon, they would arrive at the ranger's station. This afternoon? No, it would be more like forty minutes, at the most—and then there would be phone calls to the editor, mother and fiancée.

In another twenty-four hours or less—much less, because undoubtedly, Mrs. Curtis would send a plane for her son tonight—yes, tonight they would be back in San Francisco. Rather, she Stacia Marshall, the bad guesser, would be back in San Francisco, and he would be in Nevada, and never the twain would meet again. And all because she had not kept her foolish mouth shut! No use to open it for excuses. No use to tell him that going back with the bikers was the last thing she wanted, unless, *unless* she told him she was afraid of motorcycles; but then, he would think her a coward. After all, he rode them himself. She looked up at him and found his face was expressionless, non-committal. However, as their eyes met, he proved that at least their minds were traveling along similar tracks. "You'll probably be back in San Francisco by this evening."

He had said, "you," not "we." The lump in her throat had increased in size. It was difficult to speak over it. "Probably," she said. "Only, I would..." She paused, swallowing again, wondering what she could provide by way of explanation.

"What?" he prompted.

"I didn't really mean that I wanted..."

The sound was much louder. "I can't hear you," he yelled.

She could hardly hear herself, for the motors were very close now, and Paul was moving toward the stream, standing as near it as possible, as two motorcycles roared into view and passed them, only to turn around and stop quickly, one above them and the other below.

The riders dismounted, and Stacia, looking at them, was, as usual, reminded of helmeted knights. They did resemble knights, with their dark plastic visors hiding their faces. There were other similarities, too. Their tight-fitting pants and jackets were made of black leather, with some sort of orange-and-yellow shield painted on their backs. These could as easily have been coats of mail, and from the armor she had seen in some museums, she knew that for every Richard the Lion-Hearted, who had been well over six feet tall, there were hordes of smaller warriors. Neither of these men was above medium height. In fact, one of them was quite short. She looked toward Paul only to see him frowning at the pair. A snatch of the conversation she had heard that morning suddenly returned to her.

"Let's hope you don't run afoul of 'em," Jeb Craik had said. He had added, *"But you look like you can lick your weight in wildcats."*

The old prospector had been suggesting that some bikers could be dangerous; of course, she knew that, knew about motorcycle gangs. Lots of them were very rough. She wished that they would raise their visors. There was something very unnerving about looking into the blank darkness beneath their helmets. Their silence was also unnerving, but she could do something about that. "Hi," she said tentatively.

"Hi," the rider about her said in a surprisingly light voice—almost a childish voice, Stacia thought.

"Hi." The other rider spoke this time, and also in a young voice, though it was deeper than the first.

"That was good riding," Paul remarked, but to Stacia's ears, his tones sounded more censorious than complimentary.

"Thanks," the two of them chorused, and laughed. A second later, they had both pushed up their visors, and the one on the higher ground took off his, or rather, her helmet; for, to Stacia's surprise, it was a young girl, who was shaking out a mane of bright-red hair. Her companion, whose hair was darker, an auburn shade, was a boy of much the same age. She guessed them to be in their mid-teens. They looked very much alike.

"You're twins?" Stacia inquired.

"Not twins," the girl replied. "I'm a year older than Joe, here. My name's Jamie—Jamie Farr. It's my real name. It would have been James, because I was supposed to be a boy, but it stayed Jamie—because they thought Mama couldn't have any more and they were ready to settle for me—only, Joe came along, and he should have been James, Jr., only it was too complicated, so he's Joe."

"And she's been trying to be James, Jr., ever since," commented her brother in some disgust.

"I beat you up here," Jamie flared.

Joe removed his helmet, revealing that his hair was almost as long as that of his sister. "You got a head start," he grumbled.

"How old are you, young man?" Paul demanded curtly.

"What's it to you, mister?" Joe gave him an insolent stare.

"None of that, stupid; mind your manners," his sister reprimanded. "He's sixteen, and I'm seventeen and a half."

"Sixteen and seventeen," Paul repeated coldly. "Both of you are certainly old enough to know better than to ride up these trails. You're roughing up the ground."

"What are you? A ranger?" Joe asked.

"I'm somebody who needs to use the trails. I don't want to break my neck walking down them."

"Lots of bikers ride up here," the boy stated.

"Not this far. If you knew anything about riding, you wouldn't either."

"I know plenty about it," Joe retorted angrily.

"You couldn't," Paul retorted. "And why are you wearing those outfits? You look like junior members of the Hell's Angels."

Brother and sister turned to each other and simultaneously burst into laughter. "Told you!" Jamie gurgled. She bent her smiling gaze on Paul. "We're glad to hear you say so."

"God, you act like he's giving you some sort of compliment," Stacia said incredulously. "They're a bunch of goons!"

"You can say that again." Surprisingly, it was Joe who agreed with her. "We don't want to be like them, but riding all over the country, the way we do, it doesn't hurt to look like them."

"No, it doesn't hurt at all," Jamie said seriously. "It's like being one of those animals that blends into the scenery—you know, like a tree frog."

"A tree frog's an amphibian," her brother corrected.

"Well, anyhow, they do blend into the scenery, and nobody gives them any trouble. Nobody gives us any trouble, either. They don't like to tangle with the Angels." She grinned at Stacia. "You looked scared."

"I wasn't." Stacia lifted her chin.

"How'd you like to go for a ride, miss?" Joe asked with a wink.

"She wouldn't," Paul said sharply. "If you two want to kill yourselves, fine, but it's not for my wife."

"Gee, mister, you're a real spoilsport, you know?" Joe glowered at Paul. "If my dad doesn't mind, I don't see why you should make a case out of it."

"Don't be rude!" Jamie reprimanded.

Joe grinned. "I won't say it was nice meeting you, mister." He clapped his helmet on his head and, pulling down his visor, made as if to get back on his motorcycle.

"Don't be crazy." Paul stepped forward hastily. "You're not going to ride down."

"You're right; he's not." Jamie grinned and put on her helmet. "He's going to walk down, like a nice little boy, aren't you, Joey?"

"Yep, I'm not that crazy. See you." Joe gave Paul a mock bow and carefully wheeled his cycle along the trail, disappearing from view around another bend.

His sister lingered a second longer. "He's an okay kid," she said. "Just a little wild."

"You both are," Paul commented.

"Nope; only he is. I just go along for the ride." She winked at him. "Dad expects me to look out for him. 'Bye."

"Goodbye." Stacia shook her head and laughed as the girl followed her brother. "Talk about brief but explosive encounters!" She added, "You did sound a bit like the heavy father, Paul."

He was still frowning. "I wonder what's the matter with their real father, letting them run wild like this. They could get killed, and it does rough up the ground. We'd better be careful where we walk. I'm sorry, Stacia."

"Sorry?" she repeated. "It wasn't your fault."

"I mean about getting down to the ranger's station. I wouldn't have trusted either of them with you."

Her heart had positioned itself in her throat again, and she felt its pounding all over her body. She thought she understood why he had been so curt with the youngsters. He had not wanted her to get any ideas about going with them. He *did* care. "I'm not in any hurry to get to the station, Paul," she said softly.

"Oh." He regarded her in silence a moment. "I had the impression you were."

She shook her head, took a deep breath and said, "The later, the better."

"Stacia..." He gave her a long look.

She smiled up at him. "You see, you misunderstood me. And I misunderstood you. I thought you were in a hurry to get back."

"No." He frowned. "I wouldn't care if we never went back."

She moved closer to him. "That's a rather extravagant statement, but I feel the same way. I..." Her words were drowned in Paul's kiss. He was breathing hard when he finally let her go. "I haven't told you what last night meant to me," he said in a low voice.

"What did it mean?"

"You were so giving...so generous. I'm not used to that."

She stared at him in surprise. "You aren't...I would have thought..."

"It's a computerized society," he said bitterly. "And on the few occasions when I thought I'd found someone I could really love—and who really loved me—invariably, I discovered she had a calculator in her head. So much for so much, the Curtis millions, you understand."

"Oh, no, Paul, I—I can hardly believe it."

"It's true," he said somberly. "But last night was different. No weights and measures. I loved loving you. I love you, Stacia."

"I love you too, Paul." Stacia's eyes were moist.

He drew a finger beneath her eye. "Tears?"

"Because I'm so happy," she murmured. "I was afraid..."

"Afraid of what?"

"You were so silent. You hardly looked at me this morning. I didn't want you to be sorry that you...that we..."

His laughter raised echoes across the clearing. "I thought you were the one who was sorry." His laughter ceased abruptly. "Stacia, we have to level with each other. Honesty's the only basis for any good relationship. And—" He broke off. "God, it is hot here in the sun. There's a shady spot." He pointed across the clearing to a small glade. "The trees don't grow so close together there."

"And I hear a stream," she said. "I will, by the way."

"What?"

"Be honest."

"I know. That's why I said it. Because basically, I know you are honest."

"Not in the beginning," she said unhappily. "In my heart of hearts, I knew that accident wasn't your fault."

"We'll forget about the beginning," he said firmly.

"But what did you think about me?" she asked.

He grinned. "I thought you were too beautiful to be such a hellion."

"Beautiful?"

"Aren't you, Miss Green Eyes?"

"I've always thought I ought to have blue eyes, given the rest of my coloring."

"I love your eyes. I love your...Come, let's get out of the sun. I think we could both do with a rest period. Don't you agree?"

"I've already agreed."

He kissed her on the cheek. "Come, then," he urged, and started across the clearing.

Following him, she wondered how it was possible to feel any happier than she did at this moment. "Oh, there

is a stream!" she exclaimed as they entered the glade.
The stream was bordered by ferns, tall grass grew beside
it and a spread of poppies brightened the ground beneath
the trees. "How beautiful," Stacia murmured as she sank
gratefully down on the cool, moist grass.

"How's your ankle?" Paul asked anxiously.

"Fine," she said. That was not entirely true, but she
had always hated dwelling on her infirmities, and it *was*
better.

Before she knew what he was going to do, Paul had
knelt and was slipping off her shoe. He propped her foot
in his lap and undid the bandage. "It looks swollen to
me." He frowned, tenderly caressing her ankle. "I
thought we'd agreed we were going to be honest."

"I am honest," she said indignantly. "It doesn't hurt
nearly as much as it did."

"Nearly as much," he repeated. "Now, that, I expect
is real honesty."

"Oh, very well, it is," she admitted, and flushed. The
mere touch of his hand was sending little thrills all the
way up her body. Her flush deepened. She was remembering last night, and vividly, far too vividly. If she were
to be entirely honest with herself, as well, she longed
to be possessed by him at this very moment.

"Stacia," Paul murmured.

"Yes." She kept her eyes on the stream.

"Why don't you look at me?"

She did not want to look at him for fear he would read
the desire printed so plainly on her face. With an effort,
she turned her gaze on him. "I'm looking at you," she
began, and paused, startled as she saw in his eyes a
reflection of her own wanting.

"The stream goes into a pool." He pointed. "It would
be refreshing to take a dip, don't you agree?"

"Very refreshing," she echoed, daring to smile at him.

"Come, then." He took off his shirt.

Stacia looked away suddenly. Undoubtedly, he expected her to undress in plain sight. She, on the other hand, wanted to move in among the trees—but that was utterly ridiculous. Certainly, she should not feel any shyness with this man, whom she had known as she had never known anyone. Matter-of-factly, she stripped off her shirt and stepped out of her jeans and briefs.

"Beautiful," he said, coming to stand beside her.

With the shadows of the leaves dappling his body, Paul looked, Stacia thought, like some forest god. He was reaching for her. Trembling, she awaited his embrace, but instead, he scooped her up in his arms. Laughing, he ran with her. With a scream, she went down into the icy depths of the pool and came up glaring at him. "Of all the..." she began, and stopped as he dove in after her, chuckling as he surfaced beside her.

"Of all the mean, inconsiderate tricks!" she spluttered. "I am freezing to death, damn you."

"You'll be warm soon enough." He gave her an unrepentent smile.

"Oh, you!" Knotting her fists, she pounded them against his chest. "You deserve...deserve..." She paused as he grabbed her hands, kissing them.

"Are you any warmer now?" he inquired.

"I am," she said, surprised. "It's like yesterday."

"Not quite." His smile widened into a grin. "Race you?" he added. "Are you game?"

"What's the use? You'll win."

"Maybe not. On your mark, get set, go..." He plunged away from her, and she shot after him, making for the opposite bank. Reaching it, she looked around her. The water formed prisms in her eyes, imbuing the trees and shrubbery with iridescent haloes. It was very beautiful, but where was Paul? She turned back to stare across the pool. "Paul..." she called nervously, with a strange sense of foreboding. "Paul!"

There was a splash, and he came up beside her, a long green vine trailing over his eyes. "You called, madame?"

She smiled, but oddly, she still felt worried. However, she managed to speak lightly. "Goodness, you look like Pan."

"I feel like Pan."

"Musical?"

"Pipes were not all Pan played...." Paul reached for her, pulling her close.

"Paul"—Stacia felt his need, but could not help gasping—"Here...in these freezing waters?"

"Why not?" His hold tightened.

Pressed against him, Stacia forgot all about the coldness of the pool, forgot everything except the incredible excitement of being with him.

"You're shivering," he whispered finally.

"Not with cold."

"Still..." He carried her out of the pool. "Shall we let the sun dry us off?"

"Um..." She twined her arms around his neck, kissing him.

"Stacia...Stacia..." he said huskily as he put her down on the grass.

"There's no sun here," she said, looking up at the trees.

"I had a better idea," he whispered, covering her with his body. "I hope you agree."

"Entirely," she told him ecstatically.

* * *

Stacia was dreaming.

"Stacia."

At the sound of Paul's voice, her dream, which had been vivid and disturbing, fled. She could not remember it. She turned and found that he was no longer lying beside her. He was pulling on his trousers. He had brought her clothes along with his, from the spot where they'd shed them. They lay in a neat pile at her feet. She wrinkled her nose at them, then looked up at Paul. "Aw-w, do we have to go?" she asked.

His expression was similarly regretful as he nodded. "We do. We have a lot of ground to cover."

She gave him an impish grin. "I thought we'd covered it . . . and very nicely, too, thank you!"

His answering smile was tender. "We have." He knelt and kissed her. "You're in my blood, Stacia. I've never felt this way about any woman."

"Joe, hey, Joe, where are you?" The call, faint and far away, obviously issued from Joe's protective sister, Jamie.

Stacia leapt to her feet and scrambled into her clothes.

"That kid!" Paul frowned. "If anyone ever needed disciplining . . ."

"She's just full of high spirits." Stacia laughed. In her present state of mind, she couldn't be disapproving of anyone. It was funny how situations changed, she though, smoothing her tangled hair with her fingers. She had been lamenting the arrival of the bikers, fearing that their appearance would hasten her return to the city. Now she was actually grateful to that pair of crazy kids, who had whizzed in and out of their lives so quickly.

"What are you thinking about?" Paul asked.

"You," she said promptly, because it was true. Everything narrowed down to Paul.

"Stacia..."

"What?"

"Nothing. I just love to say your name, remember?" He sighed. "But we do have to go."

"I know..." She rose, and was startled to see him turn away from her quickly. "What's wrong?"

"I can't look at you without wanting you." He sighed again. "But we do have a lot of walking before us."

She was equally regretful. "I know...but at least we'll have tonight."

"Yes, tonight." He smiled, then looked up at the sun. "I feel like getting up there and pushing that damned globe across the sky."

"You'd get your fingers burned," she said, giggling.

"It'd be worth it." He didn't laugh. "Ready?" he added. "Let's go." He held out his hand.

"Okay." Taking his hand, she went with him out of the glade.

"Stacia." The trail had narrowed, and Paul was ahead of her. "Watch your step here. The path is crooked, and there's a deep ditch on the right side. It wouldn't do for you to fall into it."

"I'm being very careful," she assured him.

"How's your ankle holding up?" he asked sternly, "I want the truth."

She had actually forgotten her ankle. "It's much better."

"Honest injun?"

"Cross my heart and hope to die," she said solemnly and with the appropriate gesture.

"That's great."

"I owe it all to your treatment," she told him. Moving forward, she found that they were nearing another clearing. The stream, which had changed its course, was bubbling through it. Looking at those crystalline waters, she thought of the pool. Once more a set of delicious shivers invaded her. She hoped Paul would suggest stopping again. "Oh," she breathed, "isn't it lovely here?"

"Lovely." Paul turned back to her, his glance ardent. "And if—"

Suddenly a motorcycle roared into the clearing, seemingly headed right for them. With a shout, Paul reached for Stacia, and missed. Stepping back, he disappeared from view. At the same time, the motorcycle came to a jolting stop.

"Hey, what happened to him? Gee, I didn't mean..." The rider lifted his visor to reveal Joe's paling face.

"Paul...Paul," Stacia screamed.

There was no answer. Looking frantically about her, Stacia's eyes fell on the ditch he had mentioned. Moving forward, she looked down, and screamed again as she saw that, quite horribly, Paul in fact had fallen into it. There was a thin trickle of blood running down his forehead, and there were large rocks around him. Had he also fallen *on* rocks? "Paul...Paul..." She knelt at the edge. "Oh, God, Paul, can't you hear me?"

"What'n thunder's goin' on here?"

Alerted by those harsh but familiar tones, Stacia cast a startled glance upwards, to find Jeb Craik standing at the top of the hill. "Paul..." she began, but any further explanations were drowned out as a second motorcycle roared up the hill, stopping a few paces away from Joe.

"Get outa here, you varmints," Jeb yelled. Walking down the hill, he caught sight of the ditch and, staring into it, shot an alarmed glance at Stacia. "What happened to him?"

"Joe...Joe..." Jamie leaped off her motorcycle and

ran toward her brother. "What's wrong?"

Joe didn't look at her. He had moved to Stacia's side. "He fell," he said in shocked tones. "He went and fell. I didn't mean for anything to happen to him. I only wanted to throw a little scare into him. That's all I wanted. I didn't want him to get hurt or anything." His voice rose and cracked in a frightened sob. "I didn't mean . . ." He touched Stacia's shoulder.

"Shut up, Joe," his sister ordered coldly, as she joined them. "God!" she exclaimed staring into the ditch.

Stacia barely heard their exchange, barely questioned the sudden appearance of Jeb Craik. None of that meant anything. Only Paul mattered. She edged forward. "I'm going down there," she said.

"No." Jeb Craik had joined them. "Let me have a look at him, honey. I know a little somethin' about doctorin'. 'Sides, you shouldn't try gettin' down there. It's pretty deep'n he told me you had a bad ankle."

"I d-didn't mean to hurt him," Joe said with a groan. "I only wanted—"

"We know what you wanted," Jamie snapped. "Now shut up." She turned to Jeb. "Maybe we can help you get him out of there."

He stared at her in consternation. "Jeez, you're only a couple of kids. What'n hell did you want to come up'n do . . ." He shook his head. "Never mind. First things first. Gotta have a look at him." He moved around the ditch, scanning its sides carefully. Finally, he stopped. "Looks like I could get myself a toehold here." Without further ado, he climbed over the edge and, sticking his feet in the very soft earth, he reached the bottom and stood over Paul. "Damn," he muttered.

"What is it?" Stacia cried tearfully.

"All these rocks . . . got a gash on his head. But that ain't serious. It's his ribs . . . seems like . . . gotta get a closer look."

Stacia felt as if all the breath had left her body as she watched Jeb kneel beside Paul. The old man put a gentle hand on his face and lifted one of his eyelids.

"He isn't . . . isn't . . ." Stacia couldn't finish her question.

"He's out cold," Jeb said. "Now let's look here." Gently, he eased Paul's shirt up. "Jeez," he muttered. "Got a good gash here, too."

Stacia gasped as she saw the blood running down Paul's side, and behind her, Joe let out a hoarse scream and began to cry.

"'Tain't as bad as it looks. That's just superficial, only, I hope he didn't get too much dirt into it." He frowned and probed gently at Paul's side. "I think he broke a couple ribs on these-here rocks. We gotta get him out of this ditch. I have a rope up there on Maisie. Maybe tie him around the middle an' hoist him up. . . . You two can help." He cast a stern glance at Joe and his sister.

"We'll do anything you want." Jamie looked very distressed.

"But he shouldn't be moved," Stacia said hoarsely. "Supposing his injuries are worse . . . and maybe his back . . ."

"We can't leave him down there," Jeb told her. "We gotta get him out. I don't live far from here; only, it's kinda deep in the woods. We can put him on Maisie an' take him back to my place. I can strap him up."

"But he ought to be in a hospital," Stacia said. "If only we could get to that ranger's station."

"We can get there," Jamie said eagerly. "We can get

there on the double. We'll be glad to go."

"Yeah," Joe said. "If you want the ranger to come up, I'll bring him."

"No," Stacia said. "You'd better call his mother in Las Vegas. Tell her where we are."

Jeb growled. "I'd like to bet these two young'uns don't know where they are."

"We're not sure of the location," Joe admitted humbly.

"Well, like I said, first things first. We'll get him up to my cabin'n then I'll give you directions on how you're to get to the ranger. Meanwhile, we've got to bring him outa this-here ditch."

"Please be careful," Stacia begged in anguished tones. "We're still not . . . not s-sure what's the matter with him . . ."

"Don't take on so, honey," Jeb said soothingly. "I'm sure t'ain't nothin' that can't be fixed in two shakes. You're married to a pretty healthy young fellow, far's I can see."

She started to answer him, but no words would come. Her feelings had overmastered her, and she was beyond speech, beyond even thanking Jeb Craik for his help. But, meeting the old man's wise eyes, she knew he understood.

chapter

9

"WE'LL BE BACK soon as we get an answer." Jamie stood in front of Jeb's cabin, looking anxiously at Stacia. She gave another equally anxious look at the sky which was rapidly filling with clusters of clouds. "If we get a thunderstorm," she continued, "we'll come back the minute it's over, even if we have to hike up here."

"That's kind of you," Stacia said automatically. Standing in the doorway, she listened for any sound from Paul.

"Kind?" Jamie echoed. "It's about the *least* we could do." She shot an angry look at her brother, who stood a few feet away from them, his head lowered. "I guess you're plenty mad at Joe. We know you could sue, but please, he's not really bad. And he didn't mean—"

"I know." Stacia nodded. "He got mad at Paul."

"Yes; he hates being reprimanded. It really puts his back up, but this got to him, which is all to the good, because maybe it taught him a lesson." Jamie pushed a nervous hand through her tangled hair. "Actually, it's becoming sort of a drag, having to chase after him the way I do."

"Your parents—" Stacia began.

Jamie's face twisted. "Mom died a couple years back, and Dad's been great, but he's a cameraman at Paramount, and he's on location in Mexico—so we're on our own this summer." She looked down. "He trusts us—or rather, me. And like I told you, there's no real harm in Joe. . . . I mean, there wouldn't have been if—"

"I understand," Stacia said quickly. "And I'm sorry, about your mother, that is."

"So am I," Jamie said brusquely. "She was a good kid." She laughed shortly. "I guess that sounds funny, but they were real young when they got married. She was only seventeen, and he was nineteen. Anyhow, this isn't getting us down to the ranger's station. And you say I just call the Curtis Auto Works in Vegas and I'll be put through to his mother?"

"Curtis Motors—and be sure you ask for the main office; otherwise they'll probably give you one of the agencies."

"Curtis . . . Curtis . . ." Jamie repeated. "Hey, I never thought about it, but I read about that plane going down. Everybody had the notion the two of you were dead. And there was supposed to be a wedding . . . but . . ." She paused at an ominous roll of thunder. "Gee, we'd better get going; otherwise, we'll need to walk all the way there."

"Thanks, Jamie," Stacia said.

"I hope he's going to be okay," the girl said worriedly.

"Well, at least he's showing signs of waking. I was afraid he'd had a bad concussion."

"So was I." Jamie exhaled a long breath. "Gee, to go through a whole plane crash'n be practically unhurt and then to have this happen . . ."

"Yes." Stacia nodded. "You—you'd better be on your way."

"We will. Anyhow, I'm glad there was someplace you could bring him. This was certainly a surprise."

Jamie looked at the cabin. It was a long, narrow building, and very sturdy. "Never know what you're going to find in these woods." The girl clapped her helmet on her head. "We'll be on our way." She joined her brother. "Come on, Joe."

Joe nodded and looked back at Stacia. His eyes were suspiciously red. "Sorry," he said, and, wheeling abruptly, he strode on ahead of his sister.

Stacia hurried inside, looking across the cabin to a preposterous four-poster bed with patches of gold paint peeling off carvings of cupids intertwined with roses on a dark mahogany base. Paul was lying there, and from this distance, it looked as if he had lapsed into unconsciousness again. Jeb was sitting on a chair beside him. As she reached the bed, she was aware of a strong odor of whiskey, and noted a half-empty bottle of Seagram's on the small night-table next to the bed. "You gave him—" she began.

"He come to while you was out with the kids," Jeb replied, nodding. "Was in quite a bit of pain, so I gave him some of this stuff. It'll make it easier for him—bein' half soused. He dropped right off."

"Oh, I wish I'd been here. Was he . . . did he . . . ask for me?"

Jeb nodded. "First thing. Wanted to know if you was hurt too. Told him you wasn't."

"That's . . ." Stacia paused at the sound of distant thunder. "Do you think there's going to be a storm?" she demanded anxiously.

"Might be some sort of cloudburst. Been havin' a hell of a lot of rain up here this year. But I don't think it'll last long—'taint really the rainy season. Probably'll have the sun tomorrow."

"But he ought to be in a hospital!" Stacia sighed heavily. "I mean, you've taken marvelous care of him, binding up his ribs and all, but if there's a chance of infection from the cuts..."

"I hope I got all the dirt out," he said. "But if they don't come today, they'll be here tomorrow—that is, if you're sure they'll be sendin' a 'copter."

"I'm sure of it," she said.

"Well, if we can depend on them two young varmints..."

"I'm sure of that too."

"Them bikers is all crazy," he growled. "If they don't show, I'll go down tomorrow."

Stacia said anxiously, "I think they'll do as they promised."

"Don't trust none of 'em. Only I'm glad they turned out to be a couple of kids. I heard 'em from where I was...I was worried you'd run into some of the older ones...that's why I come."

"I don't know what we'd have done without you," she said gratefully. "And...oh, dear." She glanced up nervously at a huge clap of thunder.

Jeb rose and walked to a window. "Lots of thunderheads, an' it's gettin' ready to let loose. I don't think it'll last long, though. Guess I'll make us some soup." He gave her a measuring look. "Why don't you lie down'n get some rest, young lady. You look pretty frazzled."

"I'd rather stay here beside him." She sat down in Jeb's chair.

"Nothin' to keep you from lyin' beside him. It's a big bed." He grinned. "Come from a whorehouse down Mariposa way. I got it cheap. They was pullin' up stakes. I don't mean the madam. She an' her girls'd gone long ago. It was just a roomin' house'n they found this up in the attic."

In spite of her worry over Paul, Stacia found that she could laugh. "I guess that's why it was painted gold."

"Guess so . . . guess they wanted it to look more Frenchified. There was a bureau with cupids carved on it like these here." He pointed to the headboard. "I couldn't manage that, though. Only had a small pickup truck."

"How did you get it all the way up here?" Stacia asked curiously.

"Maisie helped. And . . ." He paused as Paul muttered and turned on the pillows. Moving to the bed, Jeb gently pushed him down. "Better he don't toss around so much—with his ribs'n all. It'd be good if you *did* try to lie alongside him, honey. Hold him down, sort of . . ."

"I will . . . oh." She looked up as she heard raindrops on the places where the cabin roof had been patched with slabs of tin.

"Yeah, its started," Jeb said. "Heavy, too. Heavier it is, the quicker it's over."

She nodded, realizing that he was more interested in comforting her than in telling her the truth. From her own experiences in the last few days, she knew there was no predicting how long the rain would last. Moving around the bed, she climbed onto it and edged closer to Paul. Staring down at him, she found lines of pain on his face. Tears filled her eyes. It seemed incredible that this calamity had struck him, and just when they were so happy. He moved again and groaned. Stacia quickly put her hands on his shoulders, gently pushing him down.

"Stacia . . ." It was only the thread of a whisper, but his eyelashes were fluttering.

"Paul, love," she said. "Are you in much pain?"

He shook his head and grimaced. His eyes opened wider, and softened as they fell on her. "No."

"You are. I'll get some more whiskey."

"No, please, no," he protested in louder tones. "I hate the stuff. You taste it?"

"No."

"I think he makes it himself out of boiled wildcats and the ground-up tusks of old saber-toothed tigers."

She could not restrain a giggle, but she sobered quickly. "You are not to talk," she said severely. "You must try to sleep."

"I'm not tired." His eyes lingered on her face. "Why are you so far away?"

"Far away? I'm right beside you."

"You're at least a foot distant. Move closer."

"But your ribs . . . you know they're broken."

"Jeb told me."

"It was so damned useless." Stacia groaned.

"Spilt-milk time, dearest," he murmured. "That kid, I guess I was hard on him, but . . ." He shook his head. "No use going over that." He stared up at the beamed ceiling. "What is this place?"

The question disturbed her. Was his mind wandering? she wondered anxiously. "It's Jeb's cabin, darling. Don't you remember?"

"I remember." A gleam of humor mingled with the pain in Paul's dark eyes. "But it doesn't resemble any cabin I ever saw. For one thing, it's so long."

"It started out as a schoolhouse," she explained. "Jeb said it was the only really good construction in town. It seems that one of the miners who came up here brought his wife. She was an extremely determined lady. She said if they were going to establish a town, they'd need to build a schoolhouse for the children, and she made some of the men construct this cabin. The paint was hardly dry when they all went away."

"Poor lady," Paul murmured.

"I can't believe she didn't end up in a schoolhouse somewhere." Stacia smiled, then added, "Jeb has fixed up this cabin wonderfully well. He even has running water in the kitchen and bathroom."

"Bathroom?" he repeated in surprise.

"He dug a well and laid the pipes himself."

"He's quite a character," Paul said admiringly.

"I don't know what we'd have done without him." She shook her head, remembering the way the old man had put Paul on the burro's back, carefully holding him there during the climb back to the cabin.

"Marines," Paul said.

"Marines?" she echoed, feeling another clutch of fear. Was he feverish, after all?

"They always land in the nick of time and save the day. Did I ever tell you I'm an old-movie buff?"

"No."

"I have lots to tell you, but it's all right. We'll have a lifetime for that, I hope."

"A lifetime?" she murmured bemusedly.

His eyes lingered on her face. "Won't we?" Before she could answer, he continued, "Please come closer to me. Let me feel you beside me, my darling."

"But your ribs," she protested faintly. Happiness was closing in on her so quickly that she was having a hard time dealing with it—a hard time trying to be sensible.

"That's my right set of ribs. The left ones are okay. I need one more here."

"One more what? Where?"

"Rib, love." He grinned. "In spite of what the liberationists say, I'm still of the opinion that all women are Adam's rib."

"Only Eve."

"You're Eve. You're everything that's beautiful, Stacia."

"Oh, Paul." She stroked his hair. "I do love you so much."

"Oh, God, I...I want to make love to you." He shifted his body and drew in a deep hissing breath of pain.

"Don't move," Stacia urged. "Please, darling, lie still." She moved closer to him. "You'll feel better soon, but you mustn't toss about so."

"When I'm better...will it be happily ever after?"

"Yes, yes, yes," she murmured.

"Do you know what you've just done, Stacia?" There was an intent look in his eyes and a serious note to his voice.

"What?"

"You've promised to marry me."

"I have?" she breathed.

"Haven't you? Or rather, will you? I'd like to be old-fashioned about this. I'd like to get down on bended knee."

"It's much better this way. And yes, my sweet, I have. I will marry you."

"Unless..."

"Unless?" she repeated with a slight sinking of the heart. Had he already changed his mind?

"Unless you'd rather not go through an official ceremony."

"It's up to you."

"I happen to like official ceremonies, on occasion—and this is one of the occasions."

"I would love an official ceremony."

"Great. We can kiss, can't we?"

"Yes." She bent over him, and a second later their lips met as, with his left arm, he held her tightly against him.

The kiss lasted a long time, but finally Stacia pulled back. "You mustn't tire yourself, darling."

"I can't think of any better way to get tired."

"Oh, Paul Curtis!"

"Yes, darling."

"Nothing. I just love to say your name."

"I'm glad you like it. You'll be using it pretty soon. Unless you're a Lucy Stoner."

"No."

"Good." His eyes closed. "Damn."

"Why damn?"

"I feel sleepy."

"Good," she said with relief.

"Love you," he mumbled. "Got to..." He slept.

Stacia drew back from him. As she did, she saw Jeb coming toward the bed. "How is he?" he asked in a low voice.

"He seems better."

"That's good." He grimaced. "I think we got ourselves a real downpour, curse it."

"You mean—you believe the rain will last?"

"Shouldn't be surprised if it don't let up until tomorrow mornin'."

"But do you think it will stop then?" she demanded anxiously.

"It should," he replied. "Looks like he's sleepin' peaceful enough. He'll be okay, honey. Another few hours won't matter much."

"I guess not," she said. "But I wish he could have something to ease the pain."

"Well." The old man grinned at her. "If I was him,

I'd be plenty glad to settle for you."

Happiness warred with anxiety as Stacia realized that if Paul could have heard Jeb's remark, he would not have hesitated to agree with him.

"Gloria... Mother... Gloria..."

Moving on leaden feet, Stacia went to the sink and, picking up another square of cheesecloth, dipped into a bowl of water. Wringing it out, she came back to the bed and placed it on Paul's forehead. His brown eyes, glazed with fever, opened wide. "Mother..." he muttered.

Stacia ran her hand through his sweat-soaked hair. "She ought to be here very soon," she said, her voice strong. "She and the doctor."

"Mother," he repeated. "Gloria, must tell... love... her," he mumbled, his eyes closing. Though his feverish muttering continued, it was not so loud or so distinct.

With a long, quavering sigh, Stacia sank into the chair beside his bed. It was midafternoon, nearly twenty-four hours since they had brought him to Jeb's cabin, since he had asked her to marry him and begged her to stay close beside him. She stifled a sob. Late last night, she had been awakened from a fitful slumber by his loud cry of "Gloria!" Anxiously bending over him, she had put her hand on his forehead and found it burning hot.

Jeb Craik, hastily summoned from his cot across the room, had shaken his head over him. "Must've gotten dirt into that cut. I was scared that might happen." He had brought a flashlight and, lifting the covers, had looked at the wound on Paul's side. Stacia winced at the recollection. It had looked so red and so swollen.

"It's infected," she had gasped.

"Yeah, don't look good. Too bad we couldn't get him into a hospital yesterday afternoon. Needs a lot of antibiotics an' stuff'n he shouldn't be tossin' around with them ribs, the way they is. Hope that damned rain lets up pretty soon."

The rain had stopped at about five in the morning— and Jeb had been ready to start down to the ranger's station. "I don't trust them young bikers," he had told her darkly. "With the ground so wet'n all, they couldn't ride up' there'n I bet neither of 'em's set foot to ground ever since they got them damned wheels."

"It's early yet," Stacia had temporized. "They might have gone; they seemed eager and sincere enough. And it would take you a long time to get there, wouldn't it?"

"Maybe most o' the day," he had admitted. "I'll give them another hour'n then I'll get crackin'." He had given her a compassionate look. "Don't worry so much, honey. He'll be okay. Once we get him back an' they pump all them medicines into him..."

He had waited until six, and then, with a detailed diatribe on the character of the two young bikers, he had left. Fortunately, he had gone no more than a mile before meeting Jamie and Joe toiling up the hill with the news that they had reached the ranger's station early yesterday evening and the call had gone through to Mrs. Curtis.

"Mother," Paul said distinctly.

"Don't worry, she's coming soon," Stacia murmured into his unheeding ears. "Jamie and Joe are down in the glade, waiting for the helicopter to land, and pretty soon your mother will be here, and they'll fly us back to San Francisco—and when you're better, you can go back to Las Vegas and...live happily ever after with Gloria."

She spoke dully. She was tired, deadly tired. She had slept for perhaps three hours in the night, but it had been a very disturbed sleep, not at all restful. Her tiredness had drained her of emotion. Later, she would have a reaction. Underneath her weariness, there was an ache in her heart, because all he had told her yesterday afternoon must have been the stuff of delirium. He had sounded lucid enough, but he could not love her. He had not called for her once, only for his mother and Gloria, Gloria and his mother.

"I must tell her." Paul sat up. He looked sternly at Stacia. "Don't you understand, Mother? I..." He groaned.

"Darling!" She eased him back onto his pillows and stroked his hair again. "Shhh, shhh, you must rest."

"But don't you see, Mother?" he demanded. "I don't feel that I can...it's as I told you long ago..." His voice trailed off wearily. "Long ago..." he whispered.

"Try to sleep, Paul," Stacia urged.

"I love her."

"I know, dear, I do. And...and you'll be with her very soon."

"Gloria," he muttered. "Now..."

"Yes, darling," she whispered, and turned quickly. She had heard the door open.

"He's in here, Mrs. Curtis." Jeb spoke in a low voice.

"Where? I don't see," a woman said.

"Over there with his missus."

Stacia turned cold. She had meant to tell Jeb the truth about their relationship, but she had forgotten. Rising hastily, she looked across the room. A tall woman in a white pants suit had entered. She was followed by a tall, grave-looking man. For a moment, Stacia wondered if the woman in white was a nurse, but as the newcomer neared her, she realized that she must be Paul's mother. There was a strong family resemblance. Both had the same dark eyes and the same strong features.

"Paul..." Without a glance at Stacia, Mrs. Curtis walked straight to the bed and stared down; then she cried, "Oh, God, Dr. Sears!" She shot a look at the man with her. "It *is* Paul. I still wasn't sure...I—I was afraid to hope." She knelt beside the bed, staring into his face. "I didn't think I would ever see him alive again. But he looks so ill. What happened to him? The girl said it wasn't the crash...a fall."

"Yes, a fall," Stacia corroborated. "Yesterday morning."

Mrs. Curtis rose quickly. Turning to Stacia, she asked coldly, "Who are you?"

Stacia did not answer. The doctor had taken Mrs. Curtis's place at the bed, and now he was putting a thermometer into Paul's mouth. "His temperature is a hundred and four," Stacia told him. "We just took it."

He glanced up at her. "I understand, but I must make my own examination."

"Who are you?" Mrs. Curtis repeated insistently.

Looking into her eyes, Stacia was amazed that, for all her emotional outburst, Mrs. Curtis's eyes were tearless, and her glance was as chill as her tone. "I—" she began.

"Those children who helped guide us up here," Mrs. Curtis interrupted, "and that old man—they've described you as Paul's *wife*." Mrs. Curtis frowned. "But I can't understand—"

"I am not his wife," Stacia interposed. "I'm Stacia Marshall, from *Eyeview*."

"*Eyeview*," Mrs. Curtis repeated. Her tone hardened. "Here for an interview already...No, what am I thinking about?" Her eyes narrowed. "You were with him, weren't you?" Without waiting for a reply, she rushed on. "It was because of you that he had to make that flight. Because of *you*," she said accusingly, and for the first time, her eyes were bright with tears.

Angry words sprang to Stacia's lips, but she did not utter them, understanding at last the effort it must have taken for Mrs. Curtis to control her emotions. Obviously, she hated displaying her feelings before strangers. It was equally obvious that for the last week, she must have been in agony. "Yes," Stacia said dully. "It was because of me . . . but it—it couldn't be helped."

Mrs. Curtis was silent a moment before releasing another deep breath. "No, I expect not. It must have been very frightening for you, too."

"Yes, it was frightening," Stacia agreed.

"Mrs. Curtis," the doctor said. "We ought to be on our way."

There was no mistaking her anxiety as Mrs. Curtis whirled in his direction. "Is he . . . is he . . . He *is* going to be all right, isn't he?"

Stacia held her breath as she waited for the doctor's answer. Was he looking worried, or was that his natural expression?

"As to that," he said, "I think we'll be able to reduce the fever. I'll give him some penicillin on the plane—but we should get him to the hospital as soon as possible."

"Of course. I'll call the attendants," Mrs. Curtis said.

"I'll get 'em." Jeb Craik spoke for the first time. Wheeling, he strode across the room and out the door.

Mrs. Curtis turned back to Stacia. "You'll come with us, Miss Marshall—and perhaps, on the way back to San Francisco, we'll talk—if we can make ourselves heard above the noise of that motor. If not, we'll speak at the hospital. I should like to know . . . to understand everything that's happened."

"Gloria . . . Gloria . . ." Paul muttered.

Mrs. Curtis stepped to his side. "Gloria's waiting for you in San Francisco, my dear. She's at the hospital." Her cold eyes were on Stacia. "She's extremely upset, very near a breakdown. She's loved Paul since they were children. And she, too, thought he was dead. It was a terrible shock—waiting to be married and hearing that the plane . . ." Her voice broke. She swallowed, and concluded, "You can imagine how she must feel, Miss Marshall."

"Yes, I can imagine," Stacia said. She turned away and was glad that she, too, could sound perfectly calm as she added, "Here's the stretcher."

"YES, I THOUGHT it must be off the hook. Thanks, operator," Stacia said slowly as she put down the telephone. For a week and a half—ever since she had found that Paul had been taken out of the San Francisco General Hospital the day after his arrival there and flown up to his home—she had been trying to reach his mother. She had left messages at Curtis Motors. She had obtained the private number at the house, but either Mrs. Curtis was "in conference" or she was "out." After her first frantic calls to his home, only to be told, by a man whom she imagined was a butler, that Mrs. Curtis was unavailable and that Mr. Curtis was too ill to speak to her, the phone had been busy. Mrs. Curtis had not done her the courtesy of calling back. The only news Stacia had had of Paul had been two short newspaper items. In the San Francisco *Chronicle*, there'd been a short piece ending with, "Paul Curtis is recuperating at home," and there'd been an item in a gossip column which described Gloria Mannon Meade's flight to Vegas to be with her ailing fiancé. It was amazing to Stacia that there had not been more news about him—especially after the headlines that had greeted their return.

Stacia shied away from remembering the hectic scene at the airport. They had been besieged by reporters. Questions had been shot at them from all sides, and microphones thrust at them. For the first time in her life, Stacia, blinking against a battery of flashbulbs, had really hated her profession. It had been practically impossible to get the stretcher through the crowds and into the waiting ambulance. And that, she reasoned bitterly, was why Mrs. Curtis was avoiding her.

"Is this your doing?" had been her incredible question when they had finally managed to escape from the press.

"Mine?" Stacia had stared at Mrs. Curtis in amazement. "Of course not."

She had met with an unbelieving stare. "Under those circumstances, Miss Marshall, who tipped them off? No outside person, save yourself, knew we were flying in."

"How *could* I have tipped them off?" Stacia had asked reasonably. "I was with you."

Mrs. Curtis had been in no mood to listen to reason. And, Stacia reminded herself, she had also been angered by what she had described as "you, posing as my son's wife." Suspiciously, she had demanded, "What did you hope to gain by that?"

"It wasn't my idea," Stacia had begun. "Paul—"

"Paul," his mother had interrupted, "you can't tell me that Paul suggested such a thing, when he and Gloria—"

"Ask him," Stacia had snapped.

Had she been that rude? she wondered. Yes; she had been beside herself with worry and she had disliked his mother on sight. Still, she wished the woman knew that she had turned down Dave Lynch's request to write an account of her experiences with the Curtis heir. He had been annoyed, was still annoyed, by her refusal, but she was too miserable to care. Mrs. Curtis's actions were no longer the main issue. By this time, Paul's fever must be down, and he must be well enough to pick up the telephone and call her himself. She fluctuated between fear and anger. Had complications set in—or did he want nothing further to do with her?

"But we were friends...if nothing else," she said aloud.

Yet, he might have had second thoughts about that. After all, in his delirium, he had called only for Gloria or his mother. She remembered what he had said about fortune-hunting women. Was he afraid that she might try to slap him with some sort of breach-of-promise suit? But nobody ever sued for breach of promise any more— that sort of action was as dead as a dodo. "If I only knew..." she muttered. But what did she really want to know? She wanted to know if he was better. She wanted to know why he had proposed to her if he still loved Gloria. And if he was going to marry Gloria, she wanted to have him explain why he'd insisted he loved her. She could not blame it on his delirium.... He had not been delirious.... She moved away from the telephone and looked blindly around her at the familiar furnishings of her small apartment, but she was not really seeing it. She was back in that wreck of a cabin—with Paul caressing her.

Her front door buzzer sounded, obliterating memories which were beginning to resemble fantasies. Stacia moved to her intercom, but as she picked up the receiver, she hesitated, wondering who was calling her. She wasn't expecting the laundry or her cleaning woman, and friends always telephoned.

"Miss Marshall," the tiny voice squeaked from the receiver, which she had not yet placed against her ear. "Miss Marshall, are you there?"

Stacia pressed the receiver to her ear. "Yes," she said cautiously. "Who is it?"

"I'm Gloria Meade. I have to see you."

In her ear, the voice did not squeak—it was cold—but the tone was urgent.

"I know I should have phoned first, but your line was busy such a long time. I would appreciate it if you could see me."

"Certainly." Stacia heard shock in her own voice. "Come up. I'm sorry—but I happen to be on the fourth floor. Four F."

"That doesn't matter," the woman said crisply. "Just buzz me in, please."

Stacia pressed the buzzer. She was still in shock as she went down the narrow hall to open her door. Standing there, she heard heels clicking on the uncarpeted stairs. Stacia smiled slightly. Like so many of her guests, Gloria Meade had started up quickly, but by the time she reached the second flight, her pace had slowed. She was breathing hard as she climbed the last three steps of the third flight, coming to a stop just beyond the top step, one hand clutching the ball that topped the balustrade, the other pressed against her heaving chest. Amazement widened her eyes as she gasped, "How...do...you...do this...every day?"

"I'm used to it." Stacia spoke guardedly.

"Better you than me," her uninvited guest said, panting. In very well-tailored jeans and shirt, a Vuitton bag in one hand and a huge diamond engagement ring on her finger, she was definitely prettier than her pictures, and she looked *very* expensive. Expensive, too, was the whiff of Patou's Joy that Stacia received when the woman finally gathered enough strength to totter into the apartment.

Passing through the narrow hall, Stacia saw her glance curiously at the pictures that covered the walls—mostly paintings she had picked up from sidewalk exhibitions or from galleries near Fisherman's Wharf. Evidently, Gloria Meade was not charmed by Stacia's taste, for she winced and shifted her gaze quickly. Coming into the living room, she looked at the small piano just inside the door with some surprise. "You must have built this yourself," she observed with an assumed lightness.

"It came up through the window," Stacia answered tersely.

"An easier trip than mine!" Her lightness of voice was well done, really, but not convincing.

Questions were chasing through Stacia's head. She hardly knew what to think—but meanwhile, she had to employ a little common courtesy in this uncommon situation. "Please, won't you sit down?" She pointed to the large wicker couch and smothered a nervous grin as Gloria Meade chose to sit in the peacock chair. Maybe she preferred thrones, Stacia thought derisively. Her guest was smiling at her, but there was a brooding, even an accusing, look in her eyes.

"I guess—" She paused, evidently waiting while Stacia took a seat across from her. "I guess," she repeated, "that you must wonder why I've come to see you." She added jerkily, "Paul doesn't know I'm here. I mean, he'd be furious if he thought I'd taken matters into my own hands like this." She paused. "He's home, you know."

"I know."

"He wanted to call you . . . but he's still pretty weak."

"Is he?" Stacia had not meant to shoot the question at her, but she could not help it. "The fever . . ."

"The fever, yes. He had a rough time, but it's down, and his ribs are mending. That old man up in the mountains did a good job of first aid, I'm told. God, it must have been one hell of a ghastly experience."

"Yes," Stacia agreed. "But he's better now?"

"Physically, he's improving, but mentally..."

"Mentally?" Stacia questioned. "That blow on the head, did it—"

"No," Gloria interposed swiftly. "Nothing like that. He's perfectly sound. It's just that he's extremely disturbed about *you*, Miss Marshall." She paused. "I do want to emphasize something. I'm not only engaged to Paul. Rather, I mean that I'm not only in love with him, but I am probably also the best friend he has in the world. It's always been like that, ever since we were six and five. It was natural we'd be thrown together. Our families were close friends. But that doesn't matter; what matters is that Paul is going through hell. You see, Miss Marshall, he feels he has a commitment to you."

"A...a commitment?" Stacia's heart had started throbbing in her throat.

"Yes, and he wants to honor it." Gloria paused and exhaled a long breath, or was it a sigh? "Practically the—the first lucid thing he said to me was that our engagement was off." Her long fingers had tensed, her nails, a deep, blood red, were digging into her knees. Her whole body was stiff, and her eyes burned into Stacia's face. "You— you can imagine what that meant to me, Miss Marshall."

Stacia could imagine; knew suddenly, chillingly, that this was no marriage cum merger. Very obviously, Gloria Mannon Meade adored Paul. "Yes, I can imagine," she murmured. Did that mean she would not release him?

"I gather," Gloria said, "that you love him too."

Stacia flushed. "Yes, that's true."

"I'm glad, because if you love him, then you, like me, will want to do what's right for him." She paused, as she had so often, showing the obvious difficulty she was having in handling this conversation, this situation.

"I do want to tell you one thing. Paul is the most honorable man I know. As I explained earlier, he didn't want me to come and see you. But I don't believe that three people should be made miserable because of his quixotic sense of fair play. And we would be miserable, Miss Marshall. I, because I love him. You, because you love him. And Paul, because he loves me. He does, Miss Marshall, but he says he has asked you to marry him and as soon as he is well enough, he means to seek you out and propose again. I beg you . . ." She halted again, her large eyes filling with tears now. "I beg you—for all our sakes, don't hold him to it. Remember, you're not two on a mountain any more."

Stacia bristled. "Is that why you think he—"

"Quite frankly, yes! Paul is a normal, healthy man. Do you think that any person in his circumstances wouldn't have acted like a man? You were there. I expect you made yourself available . . . and . . . and afterwards, he felt obligated."

Stacia's hands were clenched into fists. She would have liked to shove both into Gloria Mannon Meade's eyes, but that was childish, of course! It would have been equally childish to order her out of her apartment. "Obligated?" she questioned icily.

"Yes, obligated." Ice dripped from Gloria's lips too. "You won't be able to hold him, you know. His conscience works two ways. He'll marry you, but he'll be thinking about me, thinking about what he has lost. It was that way before . . . I mean, with me."

"Before?"

"When I married Ham Meade. I rushed into that because Paul and I had had a quarrel. I didn't think he'd ever forgive me. I was young and foolish, so I thought I'd teach him a lesson, and I plunged into marriage. I'll never forget Paul's coming to me and asking me simply, 'Why did you do it, Glo?'" Her voice broke. "That was all he said, but I could see he was heartbroken. Pauline— that's his mother—told me it was the only time she'd ever seen Paul cry. And the minute Ham and I called it quits, Paul came to me. He rushed back from Paris. And"—Her voice broke a second time—"if it hadn't been for—for you and that damned magazine and P-Pauline being so scared of what you'd say... well, we'd have been married by now." Then her tone changed, and she added, "You'll never come between us. Paul might have old-fashioned ideals about chivalry, but it's me he loves. And he always will." She stood up, saying bitterly, "I guess it was a waste of time, coming up here. I don't really expect you to give him up. After all, he *is* the Curtis heir."

"I'm not interested in his money." Stacia had also risen. She stared at Gloria Meade indignantly.

"Then... if you love him..."

"I do love him," Stacia said.

"If you do, Miss Marshall, remember, it's three lives you're wrecking. But if—if you can't bring yourself to release him, I will understand. In your place, I wouldn't want to do it either. In my place, I don't want to release him, but I'll have to—if you won't. His mother won't like that. She despises you and she loves me... but I don't expect you care about her. I—I guess I'll go now." She moved swiftly to the door, hurried down the hall and went out, closing the front door softly behind her.

"We're always saying goodbye at airports." Anne Harte lifted her coffee cup and took a large swallow. She was looking at Stacia out of sleep-dimmed eyes. "But at least this is a 747 and it will stay up until you reach New

York... and then heigh-ho for Rome." She yawned, adding, "It's a little past my bedtime."

"Come." Stacia forced a smile. "You don't usually go to bed at seven in the morning."

"I got up at six," Anne reminded her.

"It was lovely of you to come down and see me off."

"I don't know when I'll see you again," Anne complained. "You're not coming back to San Francisco."

"Well, you can come east."

"Is Washington, D.C., *east?*" Anne asked. "I've always thought it was south. Wasn't there some deal about placating the South by putting the capitol there? I remember reading about it in school."

"It is south. Close to Maryland and Virginia."

"And stocked with divinely handsome young diplomats from the world over. You're going to have a marvelous time at *Eyeview*'s Washington bureau. Damn you, Stacia, you have all the luck."

"Don't I just!" Stacia replied sarcastically. "Honestly, Anne, don't you ever think about anything except men?"

"Rarely," Anne said airily before turning severe in tone. "I hope that this time, you will make the most of your opportunities." She shook her head and sighed. "Six days on top of a mountain with the Curtis heir... and he was so damned beautiful, too."

"And he was also the bridegroom of Gloria Mannon Meade." Stacia was glad she wore masking dark glasses.

"You could've changed all that, I bet. He wasn't hurt *all* the time."

"He was *engaged* all the time. Did you read about the merger going through?"

"What merger?" Anne blinked. "That was a quick change of subject, I must say."

"It wasn't a change at all," Stacia corrected crisply.

"Mannon Tires and Curtis Motors—on the first page of the financial section of practically every San Francisco paper yesterday."

"The financial page. I never read that." Anne made a face. "Anyhow, I haven't read anything about Paul Curtis merging with Gloria Meade."

"It'll probably be a quiet and unpublicized wedding this time. And..." Stacia paused as a voice rang out over the public-address system.

"Oh, that's my flight!" Stacia said, and rose hastily.

"Have a lovely time, darling." Anne kissed her. "Remember, I demand postcards from everywhere in Italy—especially Rome."

"You'll have them," Stacia promised. She hurried out of the restaurant and up the ramp to the checkpoint, with Anne close behind.

"'Bye." Anne waved.

"'Bye." Stacia put her purse, camera and tote bag down in front of the attendants, hurried through the metal detectors, collected her things and, with another wave toward Anne, headed gladly toward Gate 11—or, at least, as gladly as anyone who was leaving a large section of her heart behind her.

Taking that into consideration, she was pleased with herself. She had managed to keep her cool. Her eyes were blurred with tears, but Anne could not have seen behind her glasses. However, she might have heard a break in her voice. Yet—in spite of the fact that it was still so hard to speak about Paul to anyone, so terribly difficult to pretend she didn't give a damn about his coming "unpublicized wedding"—she hadn't given herself away to Anne. She wondered if she had been quite as successful with Dave Lynch four days ago, when she had asked for a transfer to Washington and also demanded the Italian assignment. She hurried up to Gate 11, and soon she was on the thick red carpet that led into first class. She would be there all the way to Rome, a touch of grace on the part of Dave Lynch.

She was pretty sure he had guessed the state of her mind, particularly because she had refused, hands down, to write about her mountaintop experiences. Dave knew that wasn't like her. He understood human nature. Besides, he was more than a mere editor. In the past few months, he had become a friend, and she regretted leaving his office. She liked him a lot, but she could not stay in San Francisco, and she didn't want to return to New York. Dave had told her about the Washington vacancy and recommended her for the job. She had a sneaking suspicion he had also persuaded the bureau chief to hire her.

As she slipped into her comfortable seat, it occurred to her that she had left New York because of George . . . and now she was leaving San Francisco because of Paul . . . and why would she be leaving Washington? She knew the answer to that one. She would not be leaving Washington. She would grow old and gray in Washington, because her heart was permanently closed to any other man.

She fastened her seat belt and resolutely refrained from staring out of the window. She was not Lot's wife, but if she looked back, she would be transformed into a fountain of salt tears. Closing her eyes, she put her head back against the cushions, hoping that she would sleep. Unfortunately, she didn't feel like sleeping. She felt like thinking—rather, she could not help herself from thinking—about Gloria Mannon Meade and that incredible confrontation!

Her pain was just as great as it had been when she was sitting opposite Gloria Meade in her apartment. It had been impossible for her to doubt the girl's sincerity. And what had made it more painful was the fact that Paul must have given her a blow-by-blow description of everything that had taken place on the mountain. But he had been so very tender when he'd asked her to marry him. He hadn't acted as if he was doing it out of chivalry. Still, he had been hurt in the fall, and it was very possible that he had not been in full command of his senses—more than possible, since, in the two weeks they had been back, he had made no effort to reach her.

All things considered, and looking at it logically, if he had been strong enough to describe their situation to Gloria, including more details than were absolutely necessary unless one were trying to explain matters to a very dear friend—a beloved fiancée, for instance—he would have been strong enough to call her. He must know that she had called. Actions speak louder than words, and his actions had shouted regret, confusion and, worse yet—disinterest! And was it true what Gloria Meade had said—that he didn't know she was coming to see Stacia? Maybe he had known; maybe he had even asked her to come.

Stacia blinked away another onslaught of tears. It was time to talk some sense into herself. It had taken her a mere five, or maybe four or three, days to fall in love with Paul. It certainly should not take that amount of time to get over him, but she was dismally positive that it might take much, much longer—even as long as a lifetime!

As usual, the Rome airport was crowded. Coming off the plane, Stacia's ears were assailed by a babble of conversation in a dozen different languages. She tried to feel excited, because after all, this was Rome, which she loved and which she had not seen since she was fifteen and had made the journey with her parents. But it wasn't really Rome—not here. It was an airport, and all airports were interchangeable: big, glassy, crowded and confusing.

Fortunately, Stacia knew enough Italian to get herself a porter, collect her baggage and go through customs. Consequently, it was not long before she was out in the taxi and bus area, where, to her distress, there was a long line of angry people waiting for what appeared to be one taxi. She was about to step to the end of that queue, when a tall, darkly handsome man came up to her.

"*Signorina.*" His big black eyes disrobed her with a glance. "You want taxi?"

Stacia sighed, wishing she had not decided to wear a figure-hugging, white jersey dress. She had been thinking about the heat of Rome—not some of its male citizens. Blondes, she remembered, were particularly prized. "I don't want a taxi," she lied.

A slender dark hand fastened on her arm. "*Signorina.*" The black eyes bored into her. "*Per piacere . . .*"

"*Scusi.*" She tried to shake him off. "*Io—*"

"*Signorina.*" His grasp tightened. "Taxi *grande . . .* I take you. *No pagare . . .* you understand. I spik Engleesh."

Stacia looked past him at the porter, who was studiously staring at his feet. He was a short, thin man. Her would-be taxi driver was tall and muscular. "Please—" she began.

"Stacia!" someone called incredulously.

Startled, Stacia looked up to see a tall, fair-haired young man hurrying toward her. "Stacia," he repeated, reaching her and smiling down at her. "My God, what are you doing here in Rome?"

Meeting his bright blue eyes, she said weakly, "Hello, George," and was vaguely aware that her arm was once more her own. Out of the corner of her eye, she saw her would-be cab driver stepping back into the crowd.

"My God," George repeated. "Why are you here?"

"I'm on the first leg of an assignment. And you?"

"It's a long story, but don't get a taxi. I have my car. Let me drive you wherever you're going?"

"But your wife . . ." Stacia had met Marcella only once but had had the distinct impression that she would not have appreciated George's making such an offer to another woman, friend though she might have been.

George rolled his eyes. "My wife's not here. That's part of the long story. I'll tell you about it on the way to the city. Come along." Reaching out a hand, he relieved her of her tote bag. Glancing at the porter, he asked, "Is that your luggage?"

"Yes, but—"

"I'll take it." He pressed a coin into the porter's hand. "Come," George repeated as he picked up her large suitcase. "Traveling light, as usual, I see."

She nodded abstractedly. "Yes."

"I'm over here. My car is over here, I mean." He gestured at a vast parking lot.

"I . . ." Several negatives piled up in Stacia's mouth. She was aware that it would have been better to refuse his offer, but though they had parted on far-from-amicable terms, there didn't seem any point to it—especially since he seemed disposed to be friendly. Added to that, he already had her luggage in hand, and there was that long line of frustrated people. A glance at them assured her that the group had not changed. There was also the chance that her Latin admirer might be lurking about. She had no desire to tangle with him again. Forcing a smile, she said, "That would be lovely."

George's car proved to be a small white Mercedes Benz which seated only two. He had discovered the secret of Italian driving, which was two-thirds offensive, one-third defensive and very fast at all times. However, Stacia, who knew him to be an excellent driver, was able not to cringe as he whirled out of the airport and rushed into the stream of cars headed toward the Eternal City. "There'll be a hell of a bottleneck coming into Rome," he warned. "But that won't matter. We can talk."

She bit back a smile. Translated, George's remark meant that *he* would talk. She was just as glad of that. She was also glad that, being in Europe, he probably hadn't read about her disappearance and return, but then she remembered that he had been a wedding guest. Still, he had not mentioned anything about it—and unless he had changed drastically he would have been plying her with questions if he'd heard anything. "How long have you been out of the country, George?" she asked guardedly.

"Six weeks," he responded. "We were supposed to fly back for the Curtis marriage. I expect you read about the wedding of the year."

"Yes."

"All that money," George said wistfully. "Well, anyway, we were with the Contessa Carlotta di Maestri. Before her marriage, she was one of the Borghese family. You know, the Villa Borghese?"

"I've heard of them, George," Stacia said dryly, and hid another smile. He'd always been mightily impressed by pedigrees. She had forgotten that.

"The contessa is a dear friend of Marcella's, and we were staying with her at her villa on Sardinia. . . ." He frowned. "I won't burden you with the details of our final quarrel. It was too sordid. She knew when we were married . . ." He sighed. "And of course, Denis de Valmy showed up. Marcella used to know him. And she'd said the most ghastly things about him. But she did a complete about-face, and they became as thick as thieves—which both of them are in a way—she with her collection of husbands, and he . . . five wives. You've no idea . . ."

"And that's the story," George finished as he drew up in front of Stacia's hotel.

"Um," she said, her hand on the door handle. She had listened with half an ear to the shortcomings of the soon-to-be-ex Mrs. George Lansing, Jr. "I expect she was spoiled."

"You don't know the half of it," he said fervently.

She knew better than to remind him that he had just told her the whole of it. She said brightly, "Well, I guess I'd best get out."

He frowned and cast a critical eye at the façade of her hotel. "I don't see why you're staying at the Albergo di San Giorgio . . . it's too damned near the Scala Termini— and you get all that ghastly riffraff from the station— and the prostitutes parade up and down here at all hours during the night."

"It's still a first-class hotel, George."

"Yes, but there's the Hilton and the Grand . . . the Grand is divine, and right near the Via Veneto . . ."

"I like it here," she said crisply.

He was surprised. "I didn't know you'd ever been in Rome."

She gave him an exasperated look. It was typical of George, she thought to herself. He never listened to anything she told him. She said, "We stayed here, my parents and I, when I was fifteen."

"Oh, did you? I didn't know you'd ever been abroad. They do have some good restaurants here, though."

"Trust you to know them." She laughed.

"I'd like to take you to dinner, tonight, but—"

"But you are otherwise occupied," she said finishing the sentence for him. "I do understand."

"No, I'm not." He flushed.

"George, you're not broke?" Stacia asked bluntly.

He grinned sheepishly. "I have my American Express and my Visa cards. Marcella hasn't gotten around to . . . er . . . well, I have them, but they're pretty well extended. I'm expecting a check from home, but this is a thin week. If you wouldn't mind going Dutch . . ." He paused, then frowned hard as Stacia threw back her head and laughed. "What's funny?" he demanded indignantly.

"It's like old times," she answered, gurgling.

He managed a laugh. "You can say that again, but actually, it's different, Stacia, because I have a job coming up."

She stopped laughing abruptly and stared at him. "A . . . a job?"

He nodded. "You don't need to look as if you'd been hit by a brick."

"That's how I feel."

"Okay, I guess I deserve that. Anyhow, I'm signed for a movie. It starts next week. We're going on location to Greece."

He had spoken so casually that it took a minute for his words to sink in. "A m-movie? You—you're going to be an actor!" Stacia exclaimed.

He nodded and blushed. "I have a friend who knows somebody, and . . . well, it turns out they need a tall blond American for the second lead. I fill the bill."

"But—but you've never acted."

"On the contrary," he said bitterly, "I've done some

great acting. One of my best bits was when I told Marcella I loved her. Anyhow, I won't need to act much this time. It'll be dubbed. Both in Italian and English—if it ever gets overseas." He grinned wryly. "It's a living."

"My God," Stacia said excitedly, "you might end up in Hollywood!"

"My agent thinks its possible," he said seriously. "He says all I need's the footage."

"You have an agent?"

He nodded. "It seemed the best thing to do. Otherwise, they can screw you on the contracts. What's so funny?"

"You sound like all the actors I've ever interviewed," she told him. "You should do well."

"You have to protect your interests."

"I agree," she assured him.

"Oh. Well, be that as it may, Stacia, I would love it if you came to dinner with me—as I told you, I'm broke this week, but I do have the car, and we could drive around a bit . . . I expect you'd like to see Rome at night."

Rome at night. It had been incredibly beautiful to fifteen-year-old Stacia Marshall—and she did want to renew her acquaintance with the city, but with George? She did not want to go driving with him—she did not want to have dinner with him—but not because she cherished any lingering animosity. Much to her surprise, she did not feel anything for him. Not a trace of what she had once thought to be her "love" for him remained. In fact, she could not understand what she had ever admired about this rather vacuous man. Yet, he was as attractive as ever. She could imagine that, with his brand of tall, tanned good looks, he would be extremely successful in the movies. Had he always been so boring? she wondered. Or was it only that she had fallen so desperately in love with Paul that she would not have found any other man appealing or attractive even if he had been a combination of Adonis and Hercules?

Stacia gritted her teeth. She did not want to think about Paul. She could not help thinking about him, but if she were to spend her first night in Rome mooning about her hotel room, she would certainly not think about anything else. In the interests of exorcizing that persistent ghost, at least temporarily, she said, "By all means, George, and let me take you to dinner. My American Express Card is not . . . er . . . filled up."

"Well, all right"—he made a show of sounding reluctant—"but I'll make it up to you," he promised, as he had promised so many times before.

"Fine," she said, as she had said so many times before.

"Lord, Stacia." George smiled at her. "I'm so glad we met. If you only knew how much I've thought of you, and if I hadn't gone to the airport to see a friend off, we might never have run into each other. It's fate. And . . ." He paused as a chorus of horns shrilled at them. "I'd better unload this car and get you into your hotel," he told her hastily.

"Fine," Stacia repeated, and hoped he hadn't heard how much more enthusiastic she sounded now than she had moments before.

Rome at night. Stacia stood on the balcony of her hotel room, looking out over a stretch of roofs at the bulky towered shape of an ancient church. There was a warm breeze blowing, and, owing to the absence of bright lights in this sector of the city, it was possible to see clusters of stars in the darkened sky. The moon was a disappointment—it should have been huge and round, but it had shrunk to a quarter of its former self. Stacia sighed. It had been two weeks since she had seen its high white globe shedding silvery light on the fir trees. In Rome, there were pines, famous pines. Stately cypresses rose on the hills beyond the city—and under the ancient firs in the wilderness was a ruined cabin which she must forget, as she must forget everything else about that night. Would there be a time when, at some airport in Rome or Istanbul or Tunis, she would be hailed by Paul Curtis, who would join her and invite her out for a tour of the city, as George had done—and would she greet him as unenthusiastically—and would he mean as little to her as George did now?"

"I hope so," she breathed, and jumped as her telephone jingled. Crossing to the table beside her bed, she picked up the phone. *"Pronto."*

"Mr. Lansing awaits you, *signorina.*"

"I'll be right down," she said.

He was pacing about the lobby when she arrived. He had changed into what she used to call his uniform—a blue blazer, a white shirt with a Hermes scarf tucked into his collar, gray trousers, Gucci loafers. He looked, as always, rich and handsome.

His eyes widened as he saw her. Appreciatively, he said, "You look like a sea nymph. I believe that green gown is exactly the same color as your eyes."

"Thank you." Stacia forced a smile. It was silly to feel a pang because she was clad in the clinging jersey she had once planned to wear at the wedding that George, fortunately, had been unable to attend.

"Of course," he continued, "you will not be safe in Rome unless I am with you."

"Safe?"

"Beautiful girls are always in danger here."

"Gracious, George!" She laughed. "You'll turn my head."

"And that's what you're doing—turning heads in every corner of this lobby . . . or hadn't you noticed?"

Had he always ladled out compliments so speedily? she wondered. With a jolt of surprise, she found she did not remember. In the short space of two weeks and six days, George Lansing, Jr., had been erased from her mind. She could be going out with someone she didn't even know.

"Where do you want to go, darling?"

Mentally, she rejected the casual endearment. No one would ever call her "darling" in the precise way Paul had, but . . . but she must rid herself of his pursuing spectre, particularly since the man himself was pursuing Gloria Mannon Meade. When would they marry? Had they married already? Forget it. George had asked her where she wanted to go. She said, "You name it."

"What about the *Tre Scalini* restaurant in the Piazza Navona, where we can finish our meal with a dessert and espresso?"

"Tre Scalini. Oh, that does bring back memories." She smiled and then remembered the rich confection of chocolate, raisins, nuts and cake mixed with ice cream which had delighted fifteen-year-old Stacia Marshall at the restaurant. Twenty-five-year-old Stacia Marshall sighed. "The dessert I'm thinking about must have millions of calories."

"You needn't worry about calories." George's appreciative gaze wandered over her figure. "You've lost weight, I think. Why?"

Why? "I've been busy," she said hastily. "But I would love to go to the Piazza Navona and see the Fountains of the Rivers again—I've always had a passion for Bernini. . . ."

"Come along, then." He took her arm.

The dessert was just as she remembered it—delicious! Stacia and George lingered over espresso, watching the play of the water on the shoulders of the trident-bearing mermen and over the tossing manes of their mighty horses in the fountains. Afterwards, they drove along the Tiber, which was at low ebb in the summer; still, there was enough water to capture the reflections of the ancient buildings that lined the banks. George stopped the car by the bridge leading to the battered bulk of the Castello Sant'Angelo, that ancient fortress prison which had once been Hadrian's tomb. In the distance they could see the lighted dome of St. Peter's. They drove out of the city and along the Appian Way, with its ruined pillars bathed in moonlight. They came back to the circle the Coliseum and then to drive past the shattered remains of the *Fòro Romano*. Inevitably, they left the glory that was ancient Rome and came to sip cappuccino in one of the numerous outdoor cafes that lined the Via Veneto. The evening had remained beautiful, pleasantly cool for July, and the breeze, increasing into a wind, set the striped awnings fluttering all the way down the famous street.

"My Lord, did you ever see so many stars?" George asked predictably, putting his hand on her arm.

Stacia was definitely not in the mood for star-gazing or for casual caresses, especially not with George. She wanted the evening to end—and realized that she had the power to end it. She staged a yawn. "I think," she told him, "that I am feeling the effects of jet lag. We're just a short distance from the San Giorgio. I would like to go back, if you don't mind."

To Stacia's secret amusement, George looked understandably surprised, understandably miffed. The Stacia Marshall he had known eight months earlier had never expressed a wish to leave him. It wasn't even midnight yet! He said, "I suppose you've had a hectic time of it— San Francisco, New York, Rome—that's a lot of flying."

"Yes." She managed another yawn. "I'm really dead."

"Okay, I'll take you home, of course." He signaled the waiter. "But I hope we can do this again soon."

"I'm going to be pretty busy."

His surprise was heavily laced with indignation. "You won't be *that* busy."

Stacia sighed. Her eyelids *were* beginning to feel very heavy, and she was not in the mood to argue. "Well, call me tomorrow."

He looked affronted, and then his expression changed. "I understand . . . and I know it's all my fault."

"What?" She was truly confused by his statement.

"It's Marcella, isn't it?"

"Marcella?"

"Don't pretend you don't know what I'm talking about. I don't blame you for bearing grudges, Stacia. I was a damned fool. I was really crazy, ending what we had for Marcella. It was a mistake, a terrible mistake; I realized that almost immediately . . . Well, I told you what she was like. Now, being with you again, I know it was more than a mistake—it was a disaster." He leaned toward her, one arm sliding around her shoulders.

"Please, George . . ." she said crisply, slipping away from him and rising.

He rose too. "Stacia"—he looked at her pleadingly— "I know you must be bitter, but, darling, can't you give me another chance?"

"George," she said firmly, "I am not in the mood to

talk about anything now. I only want to go back to my
hotel and pass out."

"All right, darling, but we will have to talk."

She had half a mind to tell him that there was nothing
to say, that she had absolutely no interest in rekindling
an old flame. But there was something she did remember
about George. He would never take a plain "no" for an
answer; he would argue—worse than that, he would
worry a subject to death. She did not feel mentally
equipped to deal with him. "All right," said with a sigh.
"We'll talk . . . but tomorrow." She knew that he would
take her agreement to talk as a sign of capitulation, but
no matter, she would be better able to deal with him
tomorrow.

"I'll call you in the morning," he murmured. As she
had anticipated, there was a touch of triumph to the smile
he turned on her.

George found a parking place across the street from her
hotel. Coming into the lobby with her, he smiled. "Why
don't we have a nightcap at the bar?"

"No, George." She went to the porter's desk. "My
key, please."

"Your room, *signorina?*"

"Five-twenty-two."

Receiving her key from the porter, she turned back
to George. "Well, thank you . . ." she began, putting out
her hand.

He ignored her hand. "Come, kiss me good night,
darling," he said softly.

She shook her head. "Good night, George." She
moved toward the elevator.

He followed her. "I'd love to see your room."

She came to a stop. "No, George."

"Why not?"

"Please, don't be difficult. I meant it when I told you I was tired."

He gave her one of his most charming smiles. "Couldn't we be tired together?"

Stacia regarded him with amazement. Had he always been so utterly obtuse, so sure of his devastating effect upon her? Probably—and with good reason. She had always yielded, had always wanted to yield. She was extremely annoyed with that former self, who was creating so many difficulties for the new Stacia. "Look—" she began.

"Stacia," he interrupted, slipping his arm around her again. "You've enjoyed tonight, haven't you? I know you have, so why must you put on this act? Haven't I apologized? Haven't I told you I made a mistake?" His arm tightened. "Darling, you know you want to be with me—as much as I want to be with you."

"I don't," Stacia said in an angry whisper. She could feel her temper nearing the boiling point, but she loathed scenes in public places. "How can I convince you?" she muttered between her teeth as she tried to pull away from him.

"Stacia," George said firmly. "I am not going to let you go, not when I've found you again...."

"You damned well are!" Her voice had flamed with annoyance.

"Stacia, darling."

"Let me go," she said loudly. She was now beyond caring who heard her. "Can't you understand? I don't want to be with you. I—"

"Dearest." George had not yet released her, but his grip was relaxing. "Listen."

"Don't you see that the lady wants you to leave her

alone?" an icy voice inquired.

Stacia ceased struggling. She stood stone-still, staring incredulously at the speaker. "Paul," she mouthed.

George looked equally shocked. "What the blazes?" he began angrily.

"Good night, George," Paul said firmly.

George's mouth had dropped open. His eyes were wide. "But you're . . . you're Paul Curtis," he said, almost accusingly. "Marcella . . . we were invited to your wedding."

"I did not make out the guest list," Paul said with studied insolence.

George flushed. "I don't understand . . ."

"That seems to be one of your problems," Paul said curtly. "However, in the interests of clarification—this lady is my fiancée."

"Your . . . fiancée?" George repeated in a stunned whisper.

"Please go, George." Stacia spoke through stiff lips.

"You didn't tell me . . ." he began accusingly. He gave her a pained look and, turning, strode swiftly out of the lobby.

"Who was that?" Paul snapped. "And don't tell me that his name is George."

"His other name is—"

"To hell with his other name." Paul spoke curtly. "You just arrived in Rome this afternoon, didn't you? Where'd you pick him up? Or was he on the plane?"

She glared at him. "I didn't pick him up. I've known him for—for years. And if I *had* picked him up, what difference does it make to you? And why did you say I was your fiancée?"

"Buona sera, signore," the porter said to a tall man, who had just come in.

"Do we have to stand down here in the lobby? Can't we go up to your room?"

"Yes, yes, of course," she said bemusedly. That was not the proper answer, but she was all out of proper answers, and procrastinating was beyond her. Curiosity hammered through her brain, pounding, pounding, pounding. Her pulses were pounding too. She ought to have been prepared for him. If she had been prepared, she could have been cool, composed and dignified. As it was, Stacia felt as if pieces of herself were floating all over the lobby. She could not even protest when Paul seized her arm and guided her toward the elevator. As they came inside, he pressed five.

"How did you know?" she asked.

"The porter told me. I've been waiting for you."

"I . . . didn't see you when I came in."

"You only had eyes for George," he accused.

"I didn't, and . . ." She paused as the elevator door slid open.

"Key, please?" Paul held out his hand.

Stacia gave it to him. "I'm around the bend."

"So am I." He did not smile.

Coming into Stacia's room, Paul looked approvingly at the twin beds with their flowered spreads and at the small balcony. "Very comfortable," he commented. "Much more comfortable than the lobby."

"I think it's a nice lobby."

"I like it much better here," he replied. "The lobby was too damned crowded, with George."

Stacia stood with her back to the door, staring at him. "How can we be talking like this?" she breathed.

"Like what?"

"So casually, when . . . when . . ." Her eyes were suddenly full of tears. "And what are you doing here? You shouldn't be here. You can't be entirely well...your ribs..."

"They're better than they were, and to answer your question, I'm here because you're here." Then he added, "Do you mind if I sit down?"

"No, you must." She pulled back the spread on the bed nearest her. "Here."

"Thank you." He propped two pillows against the headboard and sat down, leaning on them. "It's very comfortable. Won't you join me?"

She was suddenly angry—almost as angry as she had been at George—at his casual assumption that, in spite of all that had happened, she was his for the asking. "What about Gloria?" she demanded coldly.

His dark eyes suddenly gleamed with fury. "Damn Gloria," he said explosively. He rose and came to her. "I wish she knew your friend George. They'd be soul mates, unable to understand when they weren't wanted."

"She came to see me," Stacia began.

"I know. She told me."

"I know that too." Stacia felt a painful throb in the region of her heart, remembering what Gloria had said about her discussion with him.

"How could you know that she told me?" he demanded.

"She said she had. She said you tried to talk her out of coming."

"I didn't know she was going to see you until afterwards—until she came to see me at home—to tell me she'd gotten me out of a difficult situation." His voice had hardened. "You have to understand Gloria."

"I do understand her," Stacia flashed. "She loves you."

"The hell she does!" he growled. "She doesn't want

her friends to know that she was jilted. But it wasn't a matter of being jilted. We agreed on this stupid marriage because she was upset at what had happened with Hamilton Meade and with a lot of other men, too, who turned out to have dollar signs on their minds. We could compare experiences—so we thought we'd join up. We weren't in love, but we respected each other and we thought we could muddle along together. A lot of people in our position settled for that sort of an arrangement— and we *were* friends." His lips twisted. "At least, I thought we were friends. That's why I leveled with her about you. I thought she'd understand. I'd forgotten what a selfish little beast she could be."

"She said she loved you," Stacia said. "She said you loved her."

"How could I love her, when I love you?" he asked reasonably. "You seemed to believe me up in Jeb's cabin. The spines were gone . . . don't let them grow back, Stacia."

"The spines?"

"Cactuses have spines." He ran his hand through her hair. "They also have roses."

Stacia, blinking away more tears, looked down quickly. "You didn't call me . . . you didn't answer any of my calls."

His hand dropped to his side. He wheeled away from her, saying harshly, bitterly, "That was because of the other Gloria in my life."

"The other—" she whispered.

"My mother," he rasped. "She is just as determined, just as selfish and just as ruthless as three Glorias rolled into one. As you know, she spirited me out of the hospital and brought me home when I was too doped up to argue with her—to tell her that I wanted to remain in San

Francisco so that I could see you every day. And"—fury coated his tones—"I stayed doped up. I was so damned weak from the fever that I didn't think it was surprising that I was sleeping all the time. But one day, I overheard Dr. Sears telling Mother that she was slipping me too many pain-killers—and for pain-killers, you can read mickeys. So I quit taking them. Also, Mother didn't say a damn word about your calls. What she did tell me was that she'd invited you up to stay and that you'd told her that you couldn't make it because you were on assignment in Carmel. That really got to me."

Stacia gasped. "It was a lie! I called and called. I . . ." Her voice broke. "It was a lie. She—she must really hate me. I know she holds me responsible for the crash—"

"No, she had mergers on her mind," he said roughly. "But that would have gone through under any circumstances, because Mannon wanted it, whether his daughter married me or the King of Siam. And—well, maybe Mother thought she could manipulate Gloria. She was afraid of you . . . but thank God for Mrs. Crandall."

"Mrs. Crandall?"

"She was the trained nurse they hired. She was a really good soul, who heard Mother giving you the old song-and-dance on the telephone a couple of times, and then leaving it off the hook. She told me about it, but not until I was up and around. I was angry with her for not letting me know beforehand, but she said it was against her professional ethics and she had a struggle with herself before she spilled the beans. I'm really grateful to her—on two counts. I had it out with Mother, and the end result of that is we've come to a parting of the ways. And I have turned over my captain's cap to her."

"Your captain's cap?"

He grinned. "I have never seen myself as a captain of industry. I don't give a damn about Curtis Motors, not since the company destroyed my dad. Mother loves controlling the company, and she has a right hand in the form of a manager, whom she might just marry one of these days—and I . . . Do you remember that paper I told you about? You probably don't."

"The Reno *Call?*" she asked.

"Head of the class, Miss Marshall." He smiled at her. "I've bought my friend out. I've got a lot of ideas about what I want to do with it—I called you to tell you about it, but I could never reach you on the phone."

"That must have been . . . during the last four days," Stacia said.

"It was. If I'd known you were going to take off . . . but I didn't. Anyhow, I'm going to need some new blood on the staff—a good photo-journalist, for instance, if she could bring herself to leave that new job in Washington. . . ."

"How . . . did you know about that?"

"Dave Lynch told me. I talked to him yesterday. And he told me where you were. I like him. I never thought I'd say that about the editor of *Eyeview.*"

"I like him too," Stacia said. "He's a lovely man."

"That's enough," Paul said in a chiding tone.

"What?"

"I prefer fainter praise for other men. You haven't told me if you'll accept the job, Stacia."

"You haven't given me a chance," she said softly.

"Well?"

"Yes."

"Of course, there *are* strings attached," he added.

"Strings?"

"Strings to connect you to the owner of the paper . . . or

should I call them binding ties?" He looked at her seriously. "You will marry me, won't you, Stacia?"

"Oh, yes, Paul," she murmured.

"And you don't mind a lifetime contract?"

"Oh, no, Paul, I..." Her words were muffled by his kiss. In deference to his broken ribs, she would have embraced him carefully, but when he proved to have other ideas, she did not complain.

Second Chance at Love